ANGELA D. SHELTON

Honor

Collapse Book Two

I dedicate this book to everyone who's done something they regret and can't take back. You are never alone.

Contents

Prologue   iii

1   Chapter One   1
2   Chapter Two   9
3   Chapter Three   18
4   Chapter Four   28
5   Chapter Five   37
6   Chapter Six   45
7   Chapter Seven   53
8   Chapter Eight   62
9   Chapter Nine   70
10   Chapter Ten   78
11   Chapter Eleven   85
12   Chapter Twelve   94
13   Chapter Thirteen   102
14   Chapter Fourteen   110
15   Chapter Fifteen   118
16   Chapter Sixteen   127
17   Chapter Seventeen   135
18   Chapter Eighteen   144
19   Chapter Nineteen   152
20   Chapter Twenty   157
21   Chapter Twenty-One   166
22   Chapter Twenty-Two   174
23   Chapter Twenty-Three   183

24 Chapter Twenty-Four 190

25 Chapter Twenty-Five 200

26 Chapter Twenty-Six 209

Collapse Series Book 3: *Independence* ~ Chapter 1 213

Prologue

Caleb Worthington opened his eyes to nothing but blackness. He blinked twice, thinking he must not be fully awake. Still black. His head pounded with the worst headache ever. When he tried to raise his hand to massage the ache, he couldn't. Someone had bound them together.

His heart raced as his throat dried and choked him. He tried to rise, but they'd tied his feet as well. What was going on here? Where was he?

Stop. Think. What's the last thing you remember?

He'd been at market day. Mom was minding the table with their neighbor, Mrs. Boswell. Jan, Renee, and Lizzy had taken Jacob on a hunt for a lamb. Dad, Mr. Boswell, and Mr. Tilbrook were at the auction to see what price their heifers would bring in.

At least, Caleb could remember these specific details, even though he couldn't remember where he was or how he'd gotten here. He wasn't full-on amnesiac. He knew he just turned nineteen. And he had a girlfriend. Sort of.

Man, it was dark in here—and hot. Had someone stuck him into a huge oven? Like the fairy-tale witch who planned to bake Hansel and Gretel.

Okay. Now you're losing it, dude. It is highly unlikely you are in a fairy tale.

Dad would tell him to think his way out of the problem and

not go all "bull in a china shop." Time to rethink the situation. Slow deep breaths, in and out. What *did* he know about his surroundings?

He was lying down somewhere hot, bound hand and foot. The floor felt like wood, and he'd swear that was a splinter in the back of his hand. No noises offered to help him with location. Not even a breeze or other air movement, so he had to be inside something. A cabin, perhaps? Whatever it was, it had no air conditioning, but few places had electricity these days.

He squirmed and tried to sit up. Success!

Now to figure out where he was. He inchwormed a foot or so until he reached a wall. It scratched like plywood against his cheek. Perhaps a shed? But how did he land in a shed, tied up, with a massive headache? He pushed his head against the wall to steady himself and turned to use the wall to lean against. Shoot! As the back of his head contacted the wall, a raised welt throbbed. That explained the headache.

Perhaps someone was nearby, waiting for him to wake up. Should he announce he was awake by calling out? Probably not a good idea. After all, if he was tied up and someone was waiting for him, it wasn't for a surprise party. Especially with the love tap on his head.

Dad would say he should pretend to be asleep and see if he could surprise whoever showed up.

Mom would tell him to pray. She had such a deep faith. Whenever something bad was going down—whether illness, injury, or wayward actions—she jumped right in with prayer. Even when Dad needed supplication, Mom prayed for him and ignored his unbelief.

Man, it was hot in here. Wherever here was.

Caleb wasn't sure what to believe since Dad was silent in his protest against God, the exact opposite of Mom's vocal devotion. He sure wanted to believe right now, though.

If God existed, he wasn't happy with Caleb. He'd sure messed things up.

Conversely, prayer couldn't hurt anything. Especially if it was a whispered one.

"God, if you are out there listening, I could use a hand here. Not sure how I got into this wooden furnace, all trussed up like a Thanksgiving turkey. I'd sure appreciate a way out. If it's okay with you, I'm going to hold off on ending this prayer, so I'll save the amen for later, when this is over."

He put his ear to the wall and listened. Nothing. Next, he lay back down and rolled to his side to listen on the floor. Still nothing.

Shoot. This wasn't helping. He needed to think. What was the last thing he remembered doing at the auction?

Thinking hurt, but he powered through the pain. *Engage your brain, Caleb!*

He'd helped unload the heifers Dad planned to sell today. At least he assumed it was still the same day. Hard to tell in this pitch-black room.

After they'd unloaded, they'd gotten the receipt from the attendant. Since the auction was going to start soon, he'd gone to grab a seat at the highest bench overlooking the auction pit. When he'd sat down, someone joined him. Someone he was happy to see. Who?

Sweat was rolling down his brow, and his mouth was cottony dry. It was so hot. Had someone put him in here to bake him to death? Why else would they leave him in this heat with no access to water? Why tie him up and lock him in a room? It made little sense.

Who had he met up with? That had to be important.

Head hurts. Thirsty. Hot.

Emma! Figures. The word *hot* would remind him of her. With her curly blond hair and bright blue eyes, she was stunning. He could spend all day thinking about her, holding her hand, or gazing into her eyes. *Hello! Earth to Caleb. Get back to the problem, man.*

Emma had sat with him. She'd run up the stairs to say hello and then joined him through the bidding. There weren't many heads to sell today, if it was still today, so the sale had ended quickly. They'd gotten a good price for the heifers too since there weren't many to buy. Dad would be happy about that. Would be happy or was happy? The sale was over a long time ago, maybe. Was Dad looking for him now?

His legs were cramped from twisting in this unforgiving position, and his wrists were killing him. They must've used zip ties on him. The plastic dug into his skin. Soaked with sweat, he couldn't tell if the fluid on his hands was perspiration or if he was bleeding from the wounds scraped into his skin.

What happened after Emma joined him? He was happy with the sale, and she'd smiled and winked one of those beautiful blues. He'd never forget that wink. As if they shared in a secret. Maybe it was time to ask her out on an official date.

Though, come to think of it, she hadn't told him where she lived. Hopefully, it was within range of their electric golf cart. No way Dad would lend him the truck for a date.

Okay, hotshot. Stop thinking about the girl. You are in a pickle here. Focus on solutions. What would Dad do?

He worked his way back to sitting up against the wall, then caterpillar-inched his way down the side of the building. It could only help to know the size of the place and perhaps find a door or a window. If there was a window—or a door. Was it possible to have a room with no door?

Whoa. Now he was having crazy thoughts. Maybe a rest would help. He was sleepy anyway. Might as well relax for a minute.

«»

His eyelids popped open. Must have fallen asleep. It was still warm, but it didn't feel as hot. Maybe things were cooling down outside.

He wiggled around. Still zip-tied. Ugh, head still hurt too. His tongue stuck to the roof of his bone-dry mouth. With effort, he peeled his tongue free and coughed. The need for water was becoming critical. His clothes held enough perspiration to fill a glass. That much fluid coming off a body had to be replaced.

Dad taught him survival skills. "You're too smart to coddle, son. Prepare for the worst, and it may save your life."

Dad had known unprepared people who ended up dead.

Dead. Caleb shivered. That better not be him soon. Why would someone lock him up in this sweatbox? And again, who?

Think, Caleb, think. What happened after the auction? Emma was there. They were going to celebrate the excellent earnings. Something small, since neither of them had money to buy something frivolous.

Puppies. That was it. Emma knew someone who had puppies for sale, and they were going to go look at them. She loved animals and couldn't wait to show him the litter. The dealer was at the far end of the market. Odd for a dealer to put himself so far away from the crowd. The closer you were to the center, the better your business was. People didn't like to walk in the heat.

He squirmed back up to a sitting position. The movement made his head swim and the room spin. At least it felt like it was spinning. It was hard to stay spatially oriented in nothing but blackness.

Emma had taken his hand as they neared the end of the market area. Sure, she was just playing and having fun, but it felt wonderful. She grinned that beautiful smile and pulled him along. He'd have gone anywhere with her right then.

At the end of the market, she pointed out the dog breeder's van. She'd said the man couldn't afford a table spot and had the puppies on the vehicle's other side. As they ran around the van, the side door slid open. But there weren't any puppies.

He stiffened now. Someone hit him on the head from behind! He'd fallen to his knees and saw Emma standing over him. She wasn't smiling now. With her hands on her hips, she smirked.

Nothing else lingered in his memory. Until he woke up in this room—this sweatbox of darkness.

His tongue stuck to the roof of his mouth again. It felt too big to be between his teeth anymore. Or maybe his mouth was shrinking in the heat. Could a mouth shrink?

Maybe another nap.

No! He'd already slept enough.

Emma wasn't a nice person. He'd been an idiot and let a girl lead him into a trap. Dad wouldn't be happy when Caleb confessed. What was lesson number one? Always be alert to your surroundings. And lesson number two? Know who your friends are.

Well, Emma, you are off the friends list. I hope you're happy.

How was he going to get out of this mess? He didn't even

know how long he'd been here or where here was. *Think, Caleb, think!*

Voices rumbled outside the building. They were getting louder, closer. What should he do? Call for help? Who knew if they were the good guys or the bad guys? If he called out and they were the ones who put him here, they'd know he was awake. He'd lose any advantage surprise could bring.

But if they weren't who put him in here, this might be his only chance to break free. A rattling sound, like a chain being moved outside the building, decided for him. They were unlocking a door somewhere, not passing by.

Bad guys.

1

Chapter One

T*wo months prior...*
Caleb let out a deep breath, trying not to cringe as nine-year-old Jacob Dunwoody bounced around like he had pogo sticks for shoes.

"Caleb, can I drive the tractor today, please?" The kid tugged on Caleb's sleeve, then swiped a grubby hand at the red hair that had grown since his last haircut and flapped as he bobbed. Mrs. Dunwoody, Jacob's mother, better sit him down soon for a trim.

"Buddy, we talked about this, remember?" Caleb looked up at the incoming clouds, rubbing his hands together. "You aren't quite tall enough yet. If you can't sit back in the seat and still push the brake all the way to the floor, you can't drive the tractor."

Having the kid following him around some days was like playing a broken record. No—more like a puppy infatuated with his owner. Jacob had even tried to follow Caleb into the bathroom this morning. That was a nonstarter.

Caleb had grown to love the younger boy, but he was an

"

adult now. He needed a different sort of following. Perhaps someone with blond hair and curves here and there. With his own blue eyes and dark hair, a blonde would stand out on his arm. *Sigh—work to do.*

"Tell you what. Why don't you take the golf cart back to the barn and pick up the buckets to feed the steers? I'll get the hay and meet you at the feeding pens. Okay?"

Jacob's shoulders dropped, and his lips slid into a frown so deep it almost made Caleb smile. But he held it in check.

"Okay." Jacob trudged toward the golf cart, scuffing his toes in the dirt.

Jacob hated not being taken seriously, especially by Caleb or Dad. Just yesterday, Dad laughed when the boy tripped on his too-large borrowed boots. Jacob had taken it so hard they almost didn't get him to eat supper, and that's saying something. That kid could eat the entire family's meal by himself if they let him. A bottomless pit.

They'd searched for new boots at market day, but young boys were rough on clothes, including footwear. His size was scarce. Though at the rate he was growing, Mom's old boots might fit him soon enough.

Caleb climbed onto the tractor and drove toward the hay stacked in the pole barn. April arrived before they knew it, and with the fields greening up, the remaining hay wouldn't have to last much longer. The cows sure enjoyed the fresh grass. He'd put out the last of the hay this week and then clean out the barn to be ready for the new year's harvest.

He pierced the large round bale with the tractor's hay spear and lifted it into the air. With the weight of it, the tractor lurched forward. In his periphery, he saw Jacob headed to the feeding pens with five-gallon buckets stacked in the back of the golf cart. Caleb sped up to get ahead of the other vehicle.

Jacob leaped out of the golf cart and hurried to open the gate into the pen as he'd been doing for the past two months. After the tractor lumbered through, the boy closed the opening while Caleb positioned the bale over the hay ring, then lowered it into place. The steers jostled for position, wanting to get to the food without being too close to the predator wielding a knife. He cut the bindings off the bale, then backed out of the pen as the animals rushed the bale.

They reversed the gate-opening process to maneuver both vehicles out and headed to the portable grain bin. There, he approached the cart to help with the buckets.

"I got 'em." Jacob gathered the stack of pails from the back of the three-rowed cart.

The heavy pile slowed the boy's progress, but Caleb didn't dare help. Jacob took pride in every chore, always eager to do as much as he could to impress the men.

They met at the bin outlet. Caleb scooped the top bucket off Jacob's stack, plopped it under the spout, then slid open the door. Grain pulsed out of the container into the bucket. The sweet smell of the feed filled the air.

"Line them up, Jacob. This one's full."

As Jacob pulled each bucket off the stack, he lined them up in three rows of three each, then moved to the other side of Caleb to whisk the full buckets out of the way.

"I'll put the full ones in the cart. You man the chute." Stifling a sneeze at the dust, Caleb closed the bin door to stop the flow of grain into the already full bucket.

They traded spots as Jacob positioned the next empty bucket under the door and then opened it and grain rustled out.

Once they'd filled the final bucket, Jacob popped into the

passenger seat beside Caleb, and they returned to the steer pen. The boy jumped out to perform the gatekeeper duties. Then they delivered the grain to the various troughs. As soon as they left one full trough, the steers crowded in and jostled for position.

"It's almost time for lunch, buddy." Caleb slapped the kid on the back, then wiped his forearm over his own dusty forehead. "Let's drop off this last load and head in."

On their way in, the dinner bell rang from the front porch.

«»

A rowdy bunch gathered for lunch today. Not only Caleb's parents and his sixteen-year-old sister but also their live-in friends, Mrs. Dunwoody and Jacob, joined with their neighbors for the meal. Mr. and Mrs. Boswell and their sixteen-year-old daughter, Renee, as well as Mr. Tilbrook and his fifteen-year-old daughter, Lizzy, made a lively lunch crowd.

"Okay, pipe down everyone." Caleb's dad held up his hands. "I've got an announcement to make."

Caleb's stomach did a little flip, and his cheeks warmed. They wouldn't!

"That's right. We've got a special surprise today," Mom called from the kitchen.

There, someone snickered as someone else said, "Hurry, they're melting."

Then the women sang in unison, " 'Happy birthday to you…' "

Mom rounded the corner into the dining room, a white iced cake with candles stuck in it aflame. The rest of the room joined in the song, " 'Happy birthday to you…' "

Dad's huge smile crinkled his tanned cheeks as his deep voice

grew deeper with each verse. " 'Happy birthday, dear Caleb...'
"

His sister, Jan, bounced up from her chair and brought a gift from under her seat.

How'd she get that in here without me seeing it?

The group belted out the ending, " 'Happy birthday to you!'
"

The teenage girls added "And many m–m–m–ooooo–oore!" in a higher octave, dragging the last word out as if it had twenty syllables.

His face had to be three shades of red as the room erupted in hoots and clapping.

Jan vibrated with excitement, popping up and down on her toes in one of her old cheer moves. "Make a wish, Caleb."

A wish. He knew what he wanted more than anything for his nineteenth birthday. But chances were he wouldn't find it wrapped up in the box Jan held.

Flattening both palms on the wooden dining table, he sucked in a lungful of air and blew a gust toward the flames. Each of the candles went out, then a beat later, popped back to life.

Mom started laughing and clapping. "Surprise! We found some trick candles!"

The entire room erupted in laughter, including him. He rubbed at the tears seeping from his eyes. "How in the world did you find those?"

She bowed her head a bit sheepishly. "They weren't exactly new. Just new enough, if you know what I mean."

The group gathered around him with backslaps and congrat-ulations that rocked his metal chair against the area rug. Then she served the cake, giving him the first and largest piece. The dewy icing was the thickest he'd seen in a while. Buying that much sugar must have cost a pretty penny. He'd enjoy every lick off his fork.

Jan slid the gift across the table to him. "Open it. We all chipped in. Hope you like it."

As everyone leaned in closer, intent on seeing him open the gift, he enjoyed keeping his sister in suspense. They'd wrapped the box in a cloth bag with a tie on the end. He untied the cord as slowly as he could manage. A quick peek at Jan after a pause in the process told him he'd hit the mark. She continued to bounce on her toes with her hands clasped in front of her chest, her barely contained excitement about to bust loose.

"Oh, come on, Caleb." She whacked his arm, then thrust her fisted hands down to her sides. "Open it!"

He let out a chortle and opened the box.

Inside, a set of wood carving knives nestled together like steers in a shoot. He'd envied a kit like this at the market. "Oh, wow." He slid out one knife and flicked a finger along the blade. "These are amazing, guys. Thank you so much."

His whittling side gig brought in money here and there. Though he did his best to save every cent—and wouldn't have dared splurge any of his savings on the pricey kit—he wouldn't be able to afford what he desired any time soon. Perhaps never, if the economy didn't come back.

"I guess I owe you all a salad bowl or a set of serving spoons, huh?"

The group chuckled as each denied any need for repayment.

He tucked the wonderful gift under his chair. Pretty considerate since they knew he enjoyed the hobby as well as generated money from it. But if they realized what his goal was, they'd feel as defeated as he did when thinking about it.

«»

After an uneventful rest of the day, Caleb took to his favorite after-dinner spot, leaning against the rail on the back porch. Max and Luna had returned from one of their evening perimeter runs and rested at his feet. The German shepherds loved to sit with their master as he worked in the evenings. For his current project, he shaped a whistle in the form of a wolf. He'd seen an example of one years ago when the internet was still a viable source of information, and he worked to replicate its beauty and function.

Bright stars glimmered overhead whenever he looked up from his project. Maybe the woman he'd marry someday was staring up at them too. Perhaps she wished to meet him as much as he wanted to find her.

He stiffened, then bent deeper over his project as a sour flavor churned from his gut to his throat. No sense thinking of a wife until he figured out the bigger problem. He could picture it now. The big honeymoon scene—him carrying his bride over the threshold... of his parents' house. "Hi, Mom and Dad, we're home." *Not!*

Wouldn't that be the lamest proposal ever? "You're my one and only. My everything. Will you make me the happiest man ever and marry me? Join me and my family on our one-hundred-acre ranch, along with the fifty people who live here."

Now you're exaggerating, Caleb. Pull yourself together, man.

No, not fifty people, but six in this house and another five right next door who practically lived here. And there weren't a bunch of hotels open these days for their honeymoon escape. They'd be lucky if they didn't have to share a bedroom with Jacob.

He cringed, thinking of a song Mom used to sing when he was a child where the little one in a crowded bed kept saying "roll over" until everyone else fell out.

Yup, that would be him. Sharing a bedroom in an over-crowded house. Not going to happen.

He peered over the handrail at his pile of wood shavings curling into the grass and imagined the worst. Caleb—a ninety-year-old grump. Jacob—taking care of him until he died, a confirmed bachelor.

A slap on his back jolted him out of his morose mental wanderings.

Dad came up beside him, hands spread out to brace him as he leaned against the porch railing. At six five, four inches taller than Caleb, he had to bend to reach the whitewashed rail. "You've been quiet tonight. Something got your head derailed?"

"Just thinkin'. Turning nineteen makes me think about my future." Caleb used the tip of his blade to detail the wolf's eye. "I figured I'd be in college by now, dating a hot cheerleader and running down the football field on Saturdays. Televised, of course." He tried to laugh, but it sounded more like a sigh.

Dad's frame swelled up as he took in a deep breath. "This isn't what any of us planned, is it? It's been a long time since humans have had to spend the bulk of their day working to have food on the table at night." Turning from the idyllic view, he put his back against the railing. "I'm sorry you've had to grow up so quickly, son. Your life won't be like mine was. But it can still be good. In fact, I've got an idea for you."

Caleb froze his knife midstroke. He couldn't breathe with the sudden weight in his chest. Was it possible Dad knew what he wanted and could help him get it?

2

Chapter Two

Caleb tried to slow his racing heart, waiting for his father to share his thoughts. If he could've reached into Dad's head and yanked them out, he would've. "What're you thinking?"

"A man needs his own space," Dad drawled.

His heart sped back up. Dad understood. Caleb waited a beat, then another. "And?"

"I've been thinking about the attic. It's a large space. It just doesn't have a good access point." Dad massaged the back of his neck. "I may have an idea from the old days. Wealthy people used to have dumbwaiters to transport items from the various floors in their manors. We could do something like that to give you access without having to build a whole staircase."

Somehow, Caleb kept his shoulders from sloping. Sure, extra living space wouldn't be the panacea for his problems, but he wouldn't turn his nose up at having his own digs. Jacob was like a little brother, but what guy wanted to share a room with his little brother?

But one big problem held back Caleb's enthusiasm. "I

appreciate the thought, Dad. But could we manage converting the attic? Where would we get the materials? It's not like we can run down to the hardware store these days."

Dad rubbed a hand against his military-cut hair, something he'd never given up despite leaving the Army years ago. "That's the other part. Where do we locate the materials? I've seen some at market day. We'll need to be vigilant about looking for them."

"Thanks for thinking of it, Dad. I appreciate the thought, if nothing else."

Caleb returned to whittling the wolf's head as Dad headed back inside.

Even if they found all the boards, wallboard, nails, paint, and who knows what else, what good would it do to have a separate bedroom *in the house*? It still wouldn't be his. How could he expect a woman to marry him and raise a family in an attic?

«»

Caleb gathered his various projects and tucked them into a box. He hadn't gotten a lot done this week, but even though he hadn't finished the wolf, he hadn't sold all the items he'd taken last week. So he padded the space around two salad bowls and two sets of fork and spoon serving utensils. Quite a few of these had sold this year. Perhaps everyone who wanted a set had bought one, and he needed a new product. Once he finished it, he'd have to see how much interest the wolf generated.

He walked toward the carport where the golf cart waited, charged up and ready. As he passed the kitchen, his mom stopped him. "Can you please carry the canned goods out for me after you drop off your box?"

"Yes, ma'am."

Besides himself, only the women were going to market today because there were no cattle to sell. So it made little sense to take the truck. Gas was too precious a resource to squander. With the rest of the men staying home, Caleb would fill in as driver and protector.

In the third-row seat, he nestled his box between the smaller table they sold goods from and the bench seat, with plenty of room for canned goods.

Mom had lined up four boxes in the hallway to the carport, and he hefted each one, then secured them on the back seat. Rubber tie-downs ensured nothing fell out as they traveled down roads that became more hazardous and pothole-ridden every day.

With everything ready for the trip, he headed to the kitchen where Mom, Mrs. Boswell, and Mrs. Dunwoody were finishing up the after-breakfast cleaning. He leaned against the raised wooden bar and snagged a cornbread muffin from the nearby bowl. "The cart is ready whenever you are."

"Ladies, our chariot is prepared." Hazel eyes aglow, Mom swept a hand through the air as if lifting a fancy dress to curtsy. "And our knight in shining armor awaits our departure."

"Why can't I go too?" Jacob had been whining all morning and refused to quit.

Caleb ruffled the boy's hair. "There isn't enough room in the cart, and you know it. Besides, I thought you were looking forward to helping Dad with the fences. You'll be part of the men's team today. Right?"

The boy stared at his shoes, kicking his toe on the floorboards. "But I want to be with you."

Mrs. Dunwoody came up behind Jacob and turned his

shoulders toward the door. "Not another word, young man. If you don't get out the door soon, you'll miss your chance to work with the men today. Then what'll you do? Take up knitting?"

Jacob went wide-eyed. "I don't do sissy stuff."

"Then get going. Scoot!"

Just then, a horn honked outside. The men were ready to head into the pastures to find the break in the fence causing the electricity to stop flowing from the solar batteries.

The first few steps the boy took toward the door were stomps of anger, but a second honk spurred him into a trot.

The slam of the front door caused the women to giggle. Caleb rolled his eyes. Sometimes chauffeuring them was like herding a group of teenage girls. Biting into his muffin, he hung back and followed as they made their way to the vehicle and situated themselves for the twenty-three-mile ride to the Upson County Livestock barn. With him pacing the cart at fourteen miles per hour, the trip took an hour and a half there and the same to get back. Quite different from the old days. The long drive could be miserable in an open-air vehicle, but today promised pleasant weather.

Once everyone settled, he started the engine. "Shall we?"

"We shall," Mom said. "Lead on, my warrior son."

Ever since the battle on their farm, Mom enjoyed teasing him, referring to him as a warrior. Not that he minded the nickname, but he didn't feel like a warrior today, just a glorified babysitter. But he'd be happy to catch up with his friends at the auction barn, anyway. It wouldn't be a total waste of a day.

Today didn't differ from any other day. He went nowhere without his gun strapped to his belt. The marauders' attempt to take over the farm two months ago was still fresh in everyone's minds. The men were always armed and ready. Even the teenage girls wore smaller guns if they were working out of sight of the house.

Once they'd arrived and unpacked, Caleb was free to wander about the market or auction barn. The women would watch the table, including his wares. He'd check back with them every so often to ensure they were okay.

Getting away from their constant discussion would be a relief. Not that he objected to their topics, but he could only take so much talk, and they never stopped. What he wouldn't give right now for some peace.

He headed toward the auction barn to check out today's prices. The cost of beef continued to climb each week. Sure, it had seen a dip or two here and there, but it maintained its steady upward trajectory. Local beef was the only option. They said the price doubled once you got into Columbus, and in Atlanta, it could even triple. Finding the materials to start a cattle farm was difficult, so those in the business before the supply chain collapsed had an advantage.

Cool engulfed him as he stepped from the day's heat into the shade, and the rich and earthy scent of dung put him at ease. Cows called out their displeasure at being away from their fields. Their lively display vied with the ruckus of other animals for purchase such as sheep, goats, and even a few flocks of chickens added to the cacophony.

He moved up to the auction arena's top bench to take in the spectacle. A handsome bull was up for sale now. His back was long and straight, and he held his head high while he meandered into the auction pit. This fellow knew he was the biggest, baddest bull in the yard and no one was going to rush him. Not a spot of white or brown invaded his midnight coat.

Man, he'd give anything to be ready to buy his first bull right now to start his herd. Fantasies. There was just no way.

He caught the eye of a young lady entering the pit area. The blonde beauty had checked out their table a few times and asked about his whittling projects. His heart did a flip when she winked at him now. Even better, she climbed the steps leading to his top bench. Would she come to where he was or settle below?

His heart almost stopped when she paused two steps below him. "May I join you?"

He felt dry, as if his mouth were full of cotton. "Sure."

Sure? Way to go, Casanova. That's the best you could come up with? You're a real ladies' man, you are. Try again. "I'd love to have the company. We've met before, at my table. You liked my whittling, right?"

While she took the last two steps up to join him, he slid down the bench to make room.

"I'm Emma." She offered him a delicate hand. Her unpainted nails flashed—naturally pink, clean, and manicured to perfection. Thick lashes surrounded her blue eyes. No way those were fake—the lashes or the eye color. He'd seen both before, and these were real.

Her emerald-green T-shirt accentuated her golden hair. Blue jeans and cowboy boots finished her ensemble, and not a speck of Georgia red clay marred the outfit anywhere. Not a working girl then. He didn't own a single outfit without some sort of stain on it, and red Georgia clay always became the color of the day on their farm. If they picked pennant colors like the knights of old Mom was bent on teasing him about—or the football teams also, sadly, of old—his would've been red Georgia clay.

"Caleb," he said.

And now we're back to one-word sentences. Awesome. Just awesome.

Surely, he could say something witty. "I'm Caleb Worthington. I'm normally here selling. Not today, though. Today, I'm just watching to see what price beef is going for. Are you selling?"

That's better. Now he didn't sound like a reject. No need to add that the cows he sold were his family's, not his own. That could come later. Much later.

"Nice to meet you, Mr. Worthington." She winked again, squinching up her pert nose. "I'm not in the cattle business, but I enjoy the auction's fast pace. Can you understand what the auctioneer is saying?"

It had been a while since he'd paid attention to the auction itself. The auctioneer had finished selling the bull and moved on to a pair of milking goats. He kept his banter fast-paced, as usual.

"One hundred bid, now two, now two. Will ya give me two?" The auctioneer directed the repartee at the crowd on the room's left side. That must be where the goat farmers sat to share news and events, as well as try to swap animals without having to pay the auction barn sales fees.

"He's started the bidding at one hundred dollars, and that guy in the blue ball cap down there bid first. Now the auctioneer is trying to double the price to two hundred—with no takers."

"One five. Who'll give me one five?" The auctioneer had slowed the pace since there wasn't any movement. "Harvey, now come on. You know these two are worth triple this price. You don't want to miss out, do you?"

Caleb had seen this before. If the audience wasn't engaged

in the sale, the auctioneer would stop his banter to get their attention by calling out the frequent buyers. His ploy worked as the man in the green hat, Harvey, nodded one time.

"Okay, I've got one five. Now, who'll give me two?"

As the auction continued, the bids came in. Caleb had something much more interesting than a goat auction to pay attention to, though.

"You here alone today? I don't recall seeing you with anyone else at the tables."

"I'm flying solo today. My parents aren't fans of the auction barn, so they don't come in. Say it's too smelly." She waved a hand, flickering those pink nails. "But I love to see the animals. Especially when they auction off the babies. They're so stinkin' cute."

Her smile—a smile that would have lit up the entire town on a dark night—warmed the dark places inside him.

"I get it. You should see the babies when they're newborns in the fields. Especially once they figure out how to run. They're a sight to behold."

"I figured you were a farmer." Her curly blond ponytail bounced as she turned back to watch the auction pit. "Your hands give it away."

He scuffled his hands together. His short, ragged nails couldn't compare to her rounded pink beauties. Calluses made a scratching sound when he rubbed his hands together, and her tiny hands likely had never seen a shovel, pitchfork, or hay bale. Nothing about her spoke of the country life he lived.

Was that what he wanted? A pretty package for sure, but how would she handle his life?

Who was he kidding? She was knockdown, drag-out gorgeous. She wouldn't be interested in him long-term and only sat with him now from boredom.

She put one of those perfect hands on his arm and blinked those gorgeous eyes. "Earth to Caleb. Was my hand comment rude or something?"

Pull yourself together, dude. "Sorry, just thinking. Would you like to take a hike around the vendor tables? I was going to see who had some building materials. We've got a project that needs done on the farm."

She popped off the bench like she'd sat on a hot coal. "Let's go."

Then she did something amazing. She put her hand out to help him up. He grasped that tiny soft hand and rose.

Though they didn't stay connected, he knew right then that he wanted to keep that hand—and the girl it belonged to—around as long as possible.

3

Chapter Three

Caleb guzzled almost a full glass of water, which caused him to gasp slightly for air.

"It's going to be a bumper crop this year." Dad snatched a mini muffin off the smooth marble counter and popped it into his mouth. "The Fuji apples are producing as mature trees should. I was thinking they'd never put out."

They were taking a morning break to get rehydrated. With the heat today almost unbearable, Caleb appreciated the respite in the kitchen. He mimicked Dad's snatch and pop, but Mom tapped his hand when he attempted a second swipe at the muffin cache.

She cooked up a storm on hot days like today. After surviving the variant, she had limited tolerance for the Georgia heat, so Dad banned her from outside work once the temperatures hit the ninety-degree mark. "I made these to welcome the Jacksons back home."

Swallowing the last of the water, Caleb set the glass in the kitchen sink, grateful their solar power kept the AC on since the power grid rarely functioned nowadays. "Do you know when they're supposed to be here? Seems like forever since I've talked to Rob."

"They're supposed to be back today. I figured we could ride over after dinner and check." She tucked the last of the muffins in a nine-by-thirteen baking dish and snapped the travel lid onto it. "So, no more muffins for anyone. This is their welcome-home gift."

He'd had three already, and if he played his cards right, Rob would fulfill his best-buddy duties and share a couple more after they delivered the gift.

"Maybe the Jacksons will help us with the apple harvest. We'll need all the hands we can get." Dad placed his glass in the sink beside Caleb's and brushed the crumbs off his long-sleeved, lightweight, UV-protecting shirt. "Meanwhile, let's get back to work. That leak in the north pasture won't find and fix itself."

That evening, Caleb climbed into the golf cart's second row as his parents settled in on the front seat. Mrs. Dunwoody and Jacob occupied the third row.

The boy's whine grated on Caleb's last nerve. "But I want to sit with Caleb."

"Hush," Caleb's mother soothed. "You can keep your momma company for a ride to the neighbors."

A peek into the last row seat showed Jacob's arms folded around his chest. Stubborn child, that one was.

Jan hadn't yet come out of the house, and they all sat waiting. After a full minute, Dad got out of the driver's seat, opened the door to the house, and hollered in. "Jan, what's keeping you? Come on!"

The socked feet running across hardwood drew closer to the door, then stopped. "Coming."

The next long pause undoubtedly resulted from Jan getting her boots off the shoe rack and putting them on, but Caleb's patience with his sister's primping was wearing thin. With the crush she'd had on Rob since they moved next door, she spent way too much time in the bathroom playing with her hair, getting ready. When she closed the door behind her, she had on her best pair of jeans, which were only slightly stained with Georgia clay, and a shirt Caleb hadn't seen before.

"Don't you look lovely, sweetie," Mom gushed.

As Jan slid into the seat next to Caleb, he could've sworn she smelled like vanilla. They hadn't been able to get that flavoring for at least a year, so his nose must've been mistaken.

"Sorry, I couldn't find something, but I'm ready now." She fluffed her long red hair. "Let's go."

Not only did she smell fantastic but she'd also curled her hair. He couldn't remember the last time he'd seen her out of the house without a ponytail and a baseball cap crammed onto her head. Rob better look out. "You look great, Squirt." He winked and waggled his eyebrows. "The new look wouldn't have anything to do with a certain friend of mine, would it?"

"I don't know what you mean." She closed her eyes and lifted her head up and away from him. "Shouldn't I want to look nice when we go visiting our neighbors?"

"Uh-huh. *Riiiight.*"

"Can we just go?"

Dad put the cart into reverse and checked behind as he backed out of the carport. "Your wish is my command." Before facing forward and putting the cart in drive, he winked at Caleb.

When they pulled into their neighbors' driveway twenty minutes later, Mr. and Mrs. Jackson, along with Rob, were in the side yard, clearing debris from an old garden plot. All three were too thin compared to the last time they'd been together.

Mr. Jackson waved them over. "Steve, Marie, good to see you!"

After hugs and backslaps, they gathered around the fire pit that had been their go-to for parties over the years. A stack of dried oak waited for their next cookout, as if hot dogs and marshmallows were still on the menu.

Caleb punched Rob in the arm hard enough to get his attention. "You ready to beat me?"

Rob didn't need any further prompting to prepare for their knife-throwing game, a tradition at every outdoor event. "Circle 'em up."

Caleb grabbed a few leaves off a nearby tree and scratched a circle in the dirt driveway. The leaves went into the circle. He eyed his buddy. "Twenty paces?"

Rob's eye had a glint in it. His mouth widened into a grin. "Make it thirty."

Now that was a challenge. He'd need to flip the blade three times at such a distance. "Thirty, it is."

They stepped off the distance, walking away from the target area, then turning to aim. Both pulled out their ever-present pocketknives. As usual, whoever lost the last game went first. So Rob had the first crack at the game.

He took careful aim, swung his hand back and forth a few times, gauging the weight of the blade and the distance to the circle. The blade went flying, spinning through the air, and missed the circle by at least two feet. "Shoot. I'm just getting warmed up."

"My turn." Caleb elbowed his friend aside.

He twitched his wrist a few times, limbering up his throwing hand, balancing, not gripping the handle in his palm. The blade open, he extended his hand, drew it back, cocked his elbow at the correct angle, then let the knife fly. It landed inside the circle—butt first. "Close, but no cigar."

They took turns, letting the blades fly toward the target until they'd skewered each leaf and claimed them as prizes. Like last time, Caleb claimed the larger number of prizes. "Winner, winner—chicken dinner."

The chant reminded him of the carnival workers trying to convince them to play the rigged fair games. It had been too long since something as normal as an outdoor festival had occurred. The thought ruined his mood, and Rob was frowning too.

Then Rob twitched his head at Caleb, and they moved into the house, retreating to the game room. Caleb cast a longing glance at the air hockey game. Since the Jacksons hadn't installed solar, the table only worked when the power was on, and right now, it wasn't. The windows provided enough sunlight to reveal the rest of the room well enough.

The musty smell of a house too long closed up invaded the game room. Rob grabbed a ping-pong paddle and ball from the worn table and bounced the ball off the surface. "Let's go. I can still take you."

Caleb meandered to the table's opposite side and took the second paddle. Then he crouched into position to receive the first serve. "So, what have you been up to? Find anything interesting in Columbus?"

Rob served the ball, striking hard with the paddle. The ball hit his side of the table, then crossed the net over to Caleb's side. "No, man. Not much going on there at all." The ball whizzed by Caleb as he swung and missed. "We stayed with Uncle Tom and his daughter. He's got a job at the police department. Dad tried to get in but couldn't. We had to give it up and come home."

Caleb recovered the ball from behind a chair and tossed it back for another serve. "What're you planning to do next?"

Rob shook his head. "I'd love to know. It isn't like I'm heading to Georgia Bulldogs for football camp, am I?" His second serve smashed across the table as if he were trying to put it through the wall behind Caleb.

Once again, Caleb swung and missed. The ball smacked the door, then skipped across the laminate floor as he grumbled. "And not like I'm going to Alabama either."

Rob scrubbed his hand over his head and tossed his paddle onto the table where it skidded under the net and ended up on the opposite side. "Man, this is just wrong. We should be football heroes with girls dripping off our arms. Workouts in the morning before classes and parties at night in the dorms."

Caleb held no illusion that he'd make it to the pros one day, but they were both good enough to play college level. At least they'd been on track for it before the schools shut down. *So. Not. Fair.*

He flexed his arms, took two deep breaths in and out, and rubbed the tightness from his neck, razor-cut hairs bristly against his fingers. "No sense griping about it. What are we going to do?"

"I don't know what we're doing tomorrow, but I've got an idea for tonight." Rob winked and walked over to a closet. He pulled a gym bag off a closet shelf, opened it, and picked out a mason jar of clear liquid. Then presented it to Caleb with a flourish. "Compliments of my uncle's stash."

"Is that what I think it is?"

A crooked smile creased Rob's hollowed cheeks. Shaking his now-shaggy brown hair back from his forehead, he winked again. "Uncle Tom said it was an old family recipe. Tastes like rubbing alcohol, but gets the job done."

"Mom would tan my hide if she smelled that on my breath."

Rob stretched tall, puffed out his chest, and lowered his voice. "Son, are you going to claim your manhood at some point in your life? Or are you going to be a mama's boy forever?"

He twisted the cap off the jar and drank from it, dripping some off his chin before he could swipe away the excess that glugged out the sides. Then he handed the jar to Caleb.

Accepting the proffered container, he sniffed at the contents. It didn't smell like anything. What did it matter, anyway? He was an adult now, and his parents wouldn't rule his life forever. He sucked down a mouthful and began choking on the powerful drink, coughing out the fumes that burned his esophagus.

"Yeah, don't breathe when you drink." Rob rescued the jar. "It takes a little to get used to, but like I said, it does the trick."

Once the coughing subsided, Caleb caught his friend snickering and downing another gulp. "How can you drink that stuff?"

Rob handed the jar back. "This is what we get. In fact, this is *all* we've got. The variant, the shortages, the closing down of the world—it all slammed the door on our futures." He pointed to the jar. "This is one refuge we can still take."

The jar was a quarter of the way gone now, and Rob's words struck Caleb like a sucker punch. Everything they'd worked for went up in smoke as the variant burned down the world's systems. As a kid, he'd watched college football with Dad on Saturdays and dreamed of the day his family would see him on the screen.

But more than the game was gone. He'd planned to use football as his doorway into a free college education. He'd envisioned a gorgeous blond cheerleader swooning at his feet after he made the winning touchdown.

They'd graduate. He'd start his construction business building high-end homes for the wealthy Atlanta crowd. Then they'd settle down together and have three kids. First, they'd have a strapping blond boy who adored his father. Then a girl just like her mom. Who knew what a third child would bring, but it would have the free spirit his sister displayed, instead of his own introverted heart.

That was all vaporized now. He couldn't even get out of his parents' home, much less get a college degree and own his own business. Thanks to the variant, life was over before it had even begun. He took another tentative sip of the fiery liquid. It didn't burn as much the second time around, didn't burn nearly as much as the truth did, and he deepened his next pull from the jar before he handed it back to Rob.

Accepting the moonshine, Rob laughed. "I see we've come to an agreement."

Caleb just nodded, and they took turns at the drink.

"My sister still has a crush on you." Caleb snagged the jar. "She took an awful long time on her hair before we came over."

Rob wiped the dribble from his chin with the back of his hand after taking his turn. "I can't believe she hasn't found a boyfriend. Maybe I should ask her out? Would that be okay with you?"

"Sure. It's not like we have a lot of options these days." Caleb put his hand up to reject the jar this time. Legs wobbly, he slumped backward and braced his butt against the air hockey table. "I'm good, thanks. Just don't give her any of this garbage. It's pretty awful."

"Say, did anything ever come from the incident with Kacie?"

Caleb froze. He hadn't heard that name in years. No one except Rob knew the story. Caleb's gut churned over that dark time in his life he wanted to forget. If only everyone could forget, especially Rob, his only reminder.

"No, man. Let's talk about something else."

They fell silent then. It was just as well. The oddly crooked room swirled, and his fuzzy head thrummed.

Jan flounced into the room, and the jar disappeared behind a chair. She leaned on the doorpost, hip jutted to the side. "Hey, Rob."

"Hey, Jan," Rob responded with a slight slur. Or maybe it only sounded like a slur to Caleb.

She turned her attention to him then. "Dad said to tell you we're heading out soon."

"On my way, just give me a minute." He braced himself to walk to the door. Man, it looked a smidge bent—maybe more than a smidge. He'd have to concentrate on walking straight.

She left, waving a farewell to Rob before exiting with a flip of her lustrous hair.

"Gotta go, man. Come see me over at the farm sometime, okay?" Caleb clapped a hand on his friend's back, partially a farewell and partially a steadying move. "You can help me clean out the toolshed."

Laughing again, Rob waved him off.

Somehow, it had become a mile-long walk to the golf cart, but Caleb pulled it off without a hitch, even though his slow plod ended in a solid flop into the seat.

Mom looked at him funny, but said nothing.

He just wanted to get home and find a place to lie down and go to sleep. Hopefully, Kacie wouldn't appear in his dreams tonight. But he feared she might.

4

Chapter Four

Caleb opened his eyes, then slammed them shut to stave off the fire blazing in front of him. Pain shot through his retinas, searing through his head. A pounding in his skull reminded him of his moonshine indulgence.

Fuzzy memories of the prior evening came, but how he landed in his bed wasn't one of them. Again, he lifted his eyelids into slits. Great, now the burning flames were just a sunrise shining through his window. He squeezed his eyelids shut.

What an idiot. Why did he listen to Rob? He had no experience with alcohol since neither of his parents were drinkers. Back when kids at school bragged about drinking and partying, a little indulgence sounded exciting. This feeling was the exact opposite.

"Caleb! Breakfast!" Dad bellowed from downstairs.

Shoot. Not good. Mom always insisted on asking for a blessing over meals before they could eat, and she wouldn't start until everyone seated themselves. Dad was waiting to eat, and just the thought of dragging his butt out of bed right now daunted Caleb.

First things first—must open eyes. He yanked the blanket over his face and peeled his eyelids open. Still bright, but not as bad. Could he get away with wearing sunglasses at the breakfast table? *Ha. Funny one, Caleb.*

He let the blanket slide down as he rose to a sitting position. Waves of nausea rolled through his stomach, and the blanket's striped black and gold lines pulsed as if the Alabama State Hornets' mascot buzzed within it.

Pounding head or not, he had to get to the bathroom. He threw the covers off and flew out of bed, dashing toward the bathroom. The toilet rushed up to his face as he dropped to his knees and barely avoided vomiting all over the floor. He spent a few minutes with his face in the bowl before laying his head down on the cool bathroom tiles.

"Caleb! Now!" Dad bellowed again.

Just great. What had he done to himself? If this was what alcohol felt like the next day, Rob could keep it all to himself.

How was he going to get down to the table and convince his family he wasn't hungover in the worst kind of way?

Grabbing the sink for support, he peeled himself off the floor and winced at his reflection. He'd seen healthier looking dead calves. Bloodshot eyes, spittle-splattered chin, and hair like someone thrust his head into a blender. The acid smell of vomit lingered. *Disgusting.*

He gathered his toothbrush and the tooth powder Mom had made. Getting the lid off the jar was more challenging than normal, but he managed. The spearmint-flavored powder helped brush the nauseating taste away. His chest warmed. Mom was such an amazing asset with her desire to learn how to make replacements for the life necessities they could no longer purchase.

Back in his bedroom, he grabbed the jeans off the floor where he'd shed them the night before. Would Mom notice if he wore the same shirt as well? Better not.

"Caleb! Do I need to come up there and help you down those stairs?"

"Coming!" he hollered back. Ouch, that hurt. The pounding in his head amped up to a new level.

He forced open his sticky dresser drawer for a clean T-shirt, the jerky motion rocking the childhood trophy on the dresser. Arms and hands didn't cooperate as well as they should have, but he wrestled it over his head. Socks were next, but he'd get those on at the table once he was sitting down. His feet were too far away at the moment, so he jammed the socks into his back pocket.

His trek through the hall and down the stairs took Olympian strength. But he crossed the finish line triumphantly and slid into his chair at the breakfast table while the rest of his family—and Jacob and Mrs. Dunwoody—stared. Surely, his situation wasn't as obvious as it felt.

"You don't look so good," Jan said.

"Are you feeling okay this morning?" Mom frowned at him. "Do you need to go back to bed?"

Dad reached over and clapped Caleb's shoulder, jostling his off-balance body forward in his metal chair. "He'll be fine today, won't you, son?"

His father's clap shook Caleb's head, and he imagined spiders quivering on the rocking cobwebs in his brain.

He had to say something, even with his mouth still full of cotton. Forcing his lips to smile, he made eye contact with his mom. "I'm good."

Her frown deepened.

"Then let's ask God's blessing, shall we?" She held her hand out to Mrs. Dunwoody on her right and Jan on her left. He took Jan's hand and clasped his father's when it extended toward him.

Mom prayed, "Father, we thank you for the many blessings you've given us on what looks like a beautiful day ahead. Thank you for the friendships that surround us in our corner of the world and for the return of our friends, the Jacksons. Please nourish us with this food so it can sustain us through the work we face today. As a family, we want to honor you with our lives, not to bring you dishonor. Please also guide us in this. Amen."

"Amen," they chorused.

They all dug into their meal of eggs and fried potatoes. Breakfast was his favorite meal of the day, but his stomach seemed inhospitable this morning. He pecked at his food here and there, wishing Max and Luna were back from their morning run. They loved to sit under his chair and wait for bits to fall from the table. He'd gladly shovel his whole plate to them.

After breakfast, he pulled his socks on and fought off an urge to sneak up the stairs and crawl into bed.

"We'll be running the bulls through the chutes," Dad said. "Need to castrate today."

"That is after breakfast cleanup," Mom added. "It's your turn today, Caleb."

If his eyes didn't hurt so much, he'd roll them. This was going to be a rough day. *Just spectacular timing on your indulgence, buddy—spectacular.*

He rose and worked at picking up plates and scraping them clean. Mom hovered in the kitchen while Dad and Jan prepped for the workday.

Mom paused in putting potato peels into the compost bucket. "Is there something you'd like to tell me about?"

Feeling her eyes boring into the back of his head as he faced away from her, he stiffened. "No, ma'am."

She moved around to his side where he could see her and pulled her hands up to rest on her hips. "You sure about that? Something is stuck in your gut. Sharing your problems can bring relief."

It was one of those moments of truth. But how could he admit what he'd done? She'd be so disappointed. "Yes, ma'am. I'm good."

"Hmm." Her eyes narrowed. "Best not to keep your father waiting too long. Get the washer started and get out there."

"Yes, ma'am."

He finished as quickly as his fumbling fingers permitted, then headed for the door. Did Mom know what he'd done? How could she? He breathed into his palm and took a whiff. Smelled like spearmint and breakfast.

Yup. It was going to be a long day.

«»

Long didn't begin to describe how work panned out. His movements were slow and clumsy, and Dad had no mercy. They'd corralled the young bulls, and their mamas lined up along the fence separating the main herd from the corral, calling for the babies they couldn't reach.

The young bulls made their own ruckus, wanting to return to their mothers to nurse and play. Poor things. Castrating the bulls was one of his least favorite jobs, but it was a part of farm life.

His lack of speed earned him a bruise on his arm when a young bull backed out of the chute before he could close it. Another time he got the rear of the chute closed, but he'd forgotten to close the front end, so they had to chase down the bull who got through untouched. Dad glared but said nothing. A tongue-lashing would've been better than silent disapproval.

By the time they walked back into the house for supper, he regretted the incident with Rob and hoped he never saw moonshine again, much less consumed it. What a waste of a day.

Mom put the dish of collard greens on the table beside the stack of cornbread muffins. Pinto beans with a bit of ground beef mixed in rounded out the meal. It all smelled heavenly, and his growling stomach ached to be filled after a full workday on little food. The nausea had passed, and he was ready to tear into the meal.

After Mom asked the blessing, he wolfed down a muffin in two quick bites.

"Gentlemen, slow down before you both choke on your food." Dad eyed Caleb and Jacob, the boy's cheeks distended, muffin spilling out of his overflowing orifice.

Mrs. Dunwoody cleared her throat and placed a hand on Jacob's arm. "Manners, please."

Jacob swallowed his muffin and washed it down with a gulp of water. "Yes, ma'am."

Caleb slowed his pace, attempting to eat as a human should instead of a German shepherd.

Once the meal ended, he retreated to the back porch where his whittling project rested on a rustic log side table. Sitting on the matching bench, he picked up the project, then opened his knife kit. The wolf whistle was forming up nicely, but still had a way to go before he could sell it on market day.

The back door opened, and Dad stepped out. Stretching his arms, he yawned. "Got a minute to share with your old man?"

Dad's hanging eyelids and drooping mouth told of their grueling day. Caleb wouldn't look any better. He'd recovered from the indulgence, except his body was spent, more so than he normally would be.

He slid over and tipped his head to the side to indicate Dad should sit beside him. "What's up?"

Rather than taking the proffered seat, Dad moved to the white wooden handrail, gripped it, and overlooked the back pasture. After a moment of quiet, he cleared his throat. "Rough day today, huh?"

Best not to read into that. Castration day was never easy. "Yes, sir. There were quite a few to cut today."

Dad shifted to lean against the rail and shoved his hands deep into his jeans pockets. "I recall having some challenging mornings back in my Army days." Seeming to change his mind about standing, he dropped to the bench beside Caleb. "It was especially trying at daybreak after I'd been drinking the previous evening with my buddies. Know what I mean?"

Well, that did it. The cat wasn't just out of the bag—it clawed up the back of his shirt and landed hard on his head. With the headache from this morning threatening to return, Caleb rubbed at the back of his head as if he could dislodge said cat. "Maybe."

"Humph." Dad bent his neck to make eye contact, demanding Caleb do the same with the movement. "Son, making an error in judgment is one thing, but lying to those who love you is another. Want to try that response again?"

Shoot. Wrong move. His cheeks burned. "Yes, sir. I know what you mean. Rob had some moonshine he'd brought back from Columbus, and he shared it with me. It was my first time, and I didn't realize how powerful that stuff was. I guess I overdid it."

Smiling now, Dad pulled his hand back out of his pocket to clap Caleb on the shoulder. "Been there. Done that. You're an adult now, son, and I can't tell you what to do forever. But I can share my wisdom with you." He moved his hand up to Caleb's head and ruffled his hair like he'd done when Caleb was a boy of five. "Nothing good comes of getting drunk. A lot of bad can be the result. I don't recommend it to anyone. But in my house, it'll be my rules. Don't come home drunk again. Got it?"

Boy, did he ever. "Got it."

After giving Caleb's hair one last tousle, Dad stood and started toward the door. "One last thing." He stopped, one hand on the jamb, and peered over his shoulder. "Whether it's this family or the one you will have someday, the people who love you should be the ones you come to when you make a mistake. Getting your blunders aired out allows you to accept what you've done wrong and move on."

Unable to maintain eye contact, Caleb focused on the wolf whistle forming in his hands. "Yes, sir."

Dad slapped the doorjamb, then grasped the door handle, and opened the door. "I love you, son. You can always come to me."

"Love you too, Dad."

After Dad closed the door behind him, Caleb's focus on the whittling job faded. He set the piece down, got up, and moved to the handrail to survey the farm. The stars shone bright on a night with no light pollution. At least there was one benefit to the sometimes on, but often off electrical grid. Night sounds of crickets, an occasional owl hoot, and even a coyote howl brought the vastness to life. He loved living on a farm. Having his own place someday was a wonderful dream. Having a wife to share it with would be a dream he'd want to wake up to.

He didn't remember his dreams from the night prior, but Kacie probably made an appearance. She tended to when he felt guilty over anything. Bad followed bad. Would he ever be able to talk to his family about her? Grinding his teeth, he clenched his hands so tight on the handrail the wood pinched his fingers. That would be too much to unburden to anyone. He'd never be able to look Mom in the eye again.

Dad was wrong. Some things a man had to keep to himself.

5

Chapter Five

Caleb's throat was parched. The brutal heat drained him quickly today.

"Time to head in for lunch, gentlemen." Dad pulled his John Deere baseball cap off and swiped at the perspiration dripping into his eyes. "A break from this heat is in order."

The overgrown fence line they'd been clearing stretched into the horizon and disappeared down a hill. They all leaned on their bush axes, resting weary arms. Who'd believe how fast the pine trees sprouted and grew up along the pastures? Briars threaded through the underbrush, catching gloves and pant legs as they moved along the line.

"Sounds good." Mr. Tilbrook slapped at the dust on his thighs. "I'm out of water anyway and was about ready to take a header into the next water trough we came across."

Caleb took a swipe at the back of his own neck, scratching at the damp hair and slick skin. The sunny, blue-sky day caused the heat to soar into out-of-control. They'd all brought water jugs, but the morning's hard labor had drained their bottles as quickly as it had drained their stamina.

Mr. Boswell nodded to a young steer munching grass near a grove of oaks. "I could eat one of those critters raw."

Head down, Jacob shuffled beside him, his skin, even his ears, beet-red under his baseball cap, and the ax he wielded, though the smallest they had, was still longer than his arms. They'd brought him along, as he'd insisted he didn't need to do "sissy stuff" in the house with the ladies, but the poor kid was flagging in the heat. He said nothing but eyed the cart holding their tools and mostly empty water jugs.

Caleb trudged the twenty yards to the golf cart, laid his ax on the bench as he climbed in, and motored back to the group. "Pile in, men. I call dibs on the first slab of cornbread."

With them aboard, he sped the cart to full throttle. At fourteen miles per hour, the trip back to the house would take a few minutes. Though the pace was nothing compared to the truck's capability, every rock, anthill, and tractor rut they hit felt like speed bumps on a raceway. The jostling ended at the side door of their farmhouse.

As the rest piled out of the vehicle behind him, Caleb wasted no time getting to the door. The scent of fresh-baked cornbread and pinto beans made his stomach growl as the fabulous smells and laughter emanated from the kitchen.

He removed his boots and placed them on the shoe rack by the door, then hurried into the dining room where plates stacked up on the end of the table. Strange that no one had sorted them out to the individual seats yet.

Jan's voice was at her high-pitched excited level. What was up? He meandered into the kitchen as the rest of the men removed their footwear.

Lizzy and Renee sat on the kitchen barstools flanking Jan as she continued speaking, her hands moving as fast as her mouth. "I can't wait to get started. This is going to be so fun!" She grinned at him as he stepped into view. "Caleb, guess what we're going to do?"

"Does it involve a swimming pool? I'd love to cool down right now." He fake-punched his sister's arm as she rolled her eyes.

She crossed her arms, tilted her head to the side, red ponytail swinging, and pulled her lips into a sneer. "Yeah, right. I'll get right on that, big brother." Then the cheerleader in her came out, and she bounced on her chair. "We're going to start a food pantry."

"You're going to what?" Dad stepped into the room, pecked Mom on the cheek, and washed his hands for lunch.

Mom wiped the sweat off Dad's cheek with a kitchen towel, then returned the peck. "We just came up with the idea. With all the extra hands we have on the farm now, we can double the crops. Then we can use the extra to help the folks who haven't figured out basic food production."

Mom's grin spread a mile wide, and her posse all nodded like bobblehead dolls.

Mrs. Dunwoody looped her arm through Mrs. Boswell's. "That's right. God has blessed us with friends, land, and resources few others have."

Lizzy and Renee linked their arms with Jan.

Solidarity. The women had decided. No doubt how this would go. The men would fall in line once the crew had spoken.

Caleb rubbed at his grimy neck, struck again by the oddity. Mom insisted Dad was the head of the household, and yet, once she set her mind on something, Dad rarely bucked against it. Now, familiar resignation dulled Dad's eyes. First, a fleeting look of surprise because Mom had signed him up for something, then the determination that said he'd do anything she wanted.

Was that what it would be like for him someday? Whatever his wife wanted, he'd capitulate to and then brave fire and storm to get it for her? He sure hoped so. He wanted what they had.

"And we even know where we can do this." Mom waved a hand. "Remember Mrs. Lancaster's house? It would be the perfect place for a food bank."

The Boswell family had taken care of their neighbor, Mrs. Lancaster, once she'd gotten too old to drive. Her only son had moved to Atlanta, and while he visited occasionally back in the day, he'd been unwilling to leave his lucrative job to move back to Shiloh. Mrs. Lancaster, likewise, refused to move to the city and relied on her neighbors to get her to and from doctors' appointments and the grocery store.

Dad dried his hands on the towel Mom handed him before drawing himself up to his full height, facing the female throng, and crossing his arms over his chest like a grand inquisitor. "How is it you think you can take over her house without her son's permission?"

Her eyes sparkling, Mrs. Boswell stepped forward. "Before she died, she said she wished she could have done more for her son. She wanted to leave him more than her old house, but she asked us to keep the place up as best we could until he could come down to sell it. Of course, that was before everything collapsed. So, we're going to rent it from the estate."

They'd plotted this whole thing out. His stomach growling, Caleb sidestepped the foray to wash up. "Is that legal? Can you decide to rent someone else's property without their permission?"

Walking over to him, Mom slid her arm across his shoulders. "Things aren't like they used to be. If we're going to keep her house up, then it needs to be used so it doesn't fall apart." She looked at Dad as her other hand jammed her hip in her no-nonsense way. "The roof leaks. We'll need to get that patched soon. Then we'll be in and out of the house regularly with the food pantry. When it needs more repair, we'll know about it and fix it. What more could the heir want? We're doing him a favor."

As Caleb reached for the towel to dry off, Mr. Tilbrook and Mr. Boswell walked into the room, Jacob trailing them. Mr. Boswell made his way to his wife for a peck on the cheek, then to the sink to wash the sweat and dirt off his hands.

Jacob slumped like a rag doll abandoned in the dirt. "Are we gonna eat soon? I'm starving."

They all chuckled, then filed into the dining room to dig in.

«»

That evening, they trekked to Mrs. Lancaster's cottage. The musty smell of disuse permeated every room. They'd sold all the furniture and belongings upon her death, as per her will's instructions. Now, their footsteps echoed off the walls, highlighting a feeling of abandonment that crept across Caleb's skin.

As the women walked through each room, discussing storing jars, bins, and crates, Caleb wandered out the back door to a porch facing the woods resting behind the house. Like most woods in the area, these spread out in a wide expanse of planted Georgia pine.

Wretched things. The tall, thin pines invaded the native woods. Back when transportation had been cheap, the trees were a commodity. According to the man who'd sold Dad their place, it had been a tree farm until, after a clear-cut, the farmer got into the cattle business instead of replanting.

Now the forest started just yards from the house. If Caleb owned this place, his first task would be to clear out those pines and plant grass. He'd turn those trees into as many fence posts as he needed to create pastures for an Angus herd.

Quit daydreaming. It'll just sharpen the ache. No sense wishing for what you can't have.

"Caleb, come look at this," Dad thundered from the house.

After one last survey of the tree line, Caleb sprinted to see what the noise was about.

«»

The roof repair on the Lancaster house was what Caleb liked to call "a backwood hick repair." They'd brought some pine tar over from the farm, and Dad climbed up the ladder, tossed a rope down for Caleb to tie to the bucket handle, then hauled the bucket to the roof. After what felt like an eternity, they'd patched every area where the tiles had peeled back or dropped off. The result was no work of art, unless you were into abstract painting.

"Good enough for government work, I guess," Dad said. "It should keep the rain out until we can find real roofing materials."

Two turkey vultures soared by, searching for lunch, as Caleb stretched his aching back, eager to get off the hot roof. Heat waves rippled over the patchwork. "Let's get back to the house for lunch before Jacob devours our share."

"Hmph." Dad trudged over to the ladder and descended with care. "That boy should grow a foot a day with as much food as he puts away."

The crunching of acorns falling from the trees proceeded skittering squirrels in the forest next to the property. Caleb held the ladder at the top while Dad stepped his way down, lowered the bucket of tar, then descended while Dad held the ladder from below. The thought gnawing at Caleb for days freed itself as he stepped off the bottom rung. "Dad, how are we going to get the supplies we need to turn the attic into an apartment?"

Dad pulled the ladder away from the house, then carried it to the golf cart. "Been thinking about that one. I'm going to give you two steers toward the expense. You've worked hard on our farm and deserve some payment for your efforts, now that you're an adult."

Caleb's heart sped to a tippy tap. Payment? He'd never even gotten an allowance. They'd not brought on a farmhand because they couldn't afford it. Now that they had more mouths to feed, the herd had to support them all. Still, Dad was going to give him two steers. "Dad, that's amazing. Are you sure we can afford it?"

Dad clamped a hand on Caleb's shoulder, pulling his hat back from his forehead with the other hand. The dad-stare of seriousness came out, and Caleb couldn't avert his eyes. "Son, I know it's hard on you. You've missed out on so much you'd planned for." Freeing him from the dad-stare, Dad scowled at his dirty boots as if it hurt to admit all Caleb had lost. "This family can sacrifice in a small way to give you some independence. Just use it wisely."

They climbed into the cart and drove back to the house. *Use it wisely.* How far could he make two steers go in the current economy? Would it be enough to buy the supplies? Perhaps he could add more of his whittling projects.

Man, how was he going to wait for a market-day run to hunt around? This was going to be fun.

6

Chapter Six

His seatmate's inability to sit still made for an uncomfortable ride. Now Jacob bobbed around like a cork on the water after an enormous fish snagged the bait as he craned past Caleb out the truck's window. "Do you think we'll find any wallboard today?"

Mr. Tilbrook, on Jacob's opposite side, said, "I wouldn't get your hopes up, Jacob. Caleb's going to have trouble finding building materials." They rode with their windows down, letting in the scent of animal dung. "But I might know someone who has access to a stash. We'll have to wait and see."

As much as Caleb wanted supplies to get his apartment started, it would also be nice to see Emma again. He missed the days when you could pick up a phone and call a girl. Not that he'd been brave enough to do that often.

Dad backed up the truck to the cattle pen as Mr. Boswell advised from the shotgun seat.

When the vehicle parked, Jacob flipped off his seatbelt and stood, eager to get out. "Can I help with unloading today? I *never* get to help."

Jacob pushed against Caleb's knees as if he planned to squeeze past to get out the door first. Sure, he was always a ball of energy, but today, he was out of control. Someone must've found espresso and laced the boy's corn biscuit.

Caleb held his hand up to block Jacob's progress. "Hold up. Let me get out before you trample me." He snickered and then slowly opened the door, sliding one leg out teasingly to taunt the youngster.

"Ah, come on, Caleb. Get out already."

He laughed, then exited to allow Jacob to scramble out.

"Caleb, Mr. Boswell and I are heading in to talk to the owner," Dad hollered. "Get them unloaded and get the receipt. And watch the boy so he doesn't get himself trampled, please." He tossed his keys toward Mr. Tilbrook. "Park it in our usual spot?"

"Will do." Mr. Tilbrook caught the keys. "Want help unloading, Caleb?"

He shook his head as Jacob tore around the truck to the rear of the trailer. "No, we've got it."

Good thing Jacob didn't have the strength and height to open the bolts holding the gates shut on the cattle trailer. Otherwise, the steers exiting would've already flattened him. Instead, Jacob was wrestling with the bolt as the steers bawled at being cooped up.

"Let me help." Caleb stood near Jacob and waited for the boy to move aside.

Not to be deterred, Jacob gave the bolt another rough shove, putting everything he had into it, but the bolt remained in place. The kid's shoulders drooped. "I want to open it."

"Tell you what." Caleb patted Jacob's back. "I'll get it started for you, but once the bolt is up, your job is to open that gate and step back behind it so the steers can get past you to the pen. Deal?"

Jacob's face brightened. "Deal."

Caleb yanked on the rusty bolt and slid it until it barely connected to the bottom loop. He nodded at Jacob, who jiggled it free.

"Now grab that gate and move back out of the way." Caleb motioned in the direction Jacob should go.

The two steers ran their escape route as soon as the gate swung free, shaking the trailer from side to side with their enthusiasm. Once they were through the pen's opening, Caleb closed the gate, securing the rambunctious animals. "Let's get that receipt, buddy."

Jacob whooped, ready to explore.

Caleb closed the trailer doors, then waved to Mr. Tilbrook, letting him know to move the truck to the parking area.

"Can we look at the rabbits today?" Springing ahead like one of those critters ready to bolt, Jacob lurched toward the market day tables, already having forgotten about their task.

"We'll see." Caleb grabbed the boy's collar before he could bound further away. "Receipt first, remember?"

A frown crumpled Jacob's face, and his whole body sagged. He kicked at a stone. "Oh, yeah."

Getting the tokens that represented the two steers took a bit. The auction barn had done away with paper receipts after they ran out and couldn't replace them. Instead, the clerk handed out round wooden circles, about the size of quarters but much thicker. Numbers burned into them on one side, the brand of the auction house on the other. Each day, they lined the cattle up in the order they came, and the tokens represented them when payment was due.

Jacob's impatience was getting the better of him again. He'd been hopping from foot to foot during the entire transaction. When Caleb stepped away from the intake window, Jacob's eyes lit up. "Can we go now?"

"Yes, you big goofball. But we're heading to the parking lot to find Mr. Tilbrook first." Caleb ruffled the boy's hair. "He needs to introduce me to the person who has the building supplies, remember?"

"Ah, man." Jacob's shoulders drooped once more.

"If you wanted to run the auction area, you should have taken the golf-cart ride with Jan and the ladies." Caleb furrowed his brow, doing his best dad imitation. Had he been this annoying when he was nine years old? "Do you want me to take you over to the tables once the ladies get here?"

Jacob kicked at a stone in the pathway to the parking lot. "No. I'm just bored."

Mr. Tilbrook stood with a crowd of farmers who parked their trucks and trailers in the same area each week. Most likely, they discussed the current rates of grain, hay, and beef. When he saw them, he excused himself from the group and clapped Jacob on the shoulder. "Let's see if we can find a friend. You ready to help Caleb build his apartment, son?"

The boy's eyes lit up. "Sure."

Instead of heading toward the market's main table area, Mr. Tilbrook led them to the auction barn arena. Inside, they met some men Caleb had seen sitting in the lower corner each week. Seeming more interested in the local gossip than the auction, they rarely bid on the animals.

"Morning, gentlemen," Mr. Tilbrook said. When various members proffered greetings, he nodded to a man wearing blue jean coveralls and a filthy ball cap. "Wonder if I might steal some of your time, Matt."

The man excused himself.

Caleb sized him up as they meandered over to a corner area. An unkempt, gray-flecked beard and torn T-shirt said the man wasn't concerned about appearances. The bulge of his cheek revealed a lack of concern over his health. He pulled a flask out of his pocket and spit tobacco juice into it. *Disgusting.*

"What can I do you for?" Matt asked Mr. Tilbrook, but eyed Caleb and Jacob.

Mr. Tilbrook pointed to Caleb. "Meet Caleb, Steve Worthington's boy." He then gave Jacob a quick pat on the head. "And this is Jacob, a friend of the family."

Jacob smiled shyly, then scooted behind Caleb.

Mr. Tilbrook continued, "Caleb, Mr. Matt Jenkins here is the only person I can think of who might have some building supplies available."

Caleb held his hand out, and Mr. Jenkins shook it. "Nice to meet you, Mr. Jenkins. I'm looking for some basic supplies to convert an attic into an apartment, so wallboard, spackling compound… I'm sure you know what all we need."

"Hmm." Mr. Jenkins eyed Caleb up and down as if evaluating a fair sideshow specimen. "Not cheap. You got money?"

Having watched Dad negotiate, he knew never to be the first person to throw out a dollar amount. "I'm working on that part. How much do you think for an area of about nine hundred square feet?"

The flask came back out for another discharge from the man's mouth. "I'd want to see your money before I take you to see my inventory."

Now he shifted to his opposite foot, getting frustrated. "Yes, sir. I understand. Can you help me estimate the cost for my area?"

Mr. Jenkins wiped spittle from his mouth with the back of his hand, leaving a grimy streak he didn't seem concerned with. "Did some work for your father when he first bought that farm of his. Your dad's a fair negotiator. I'd need to know what interior walls you've got or will need. I can come out to your place to take measurements and give you an estimate." He fished out a tobacco container. "Mind you, I don't do drywall anymore, just provide the materials. The work's all on you."

Whew, some progress. "Yes, sir. I understand and appreciate the estimate."

They shook hands and agreed to a day Mr. Jenkins could come out. Though Caleb was no closer to knowing how much money he'd need or whether the two steers Dad had given him would cover the materials, his step was lighter.

Jacob grabbed Caleb's arm and tugged. "Come on. You said we could find the rabbits."

"You're fascinated with those animals, aren't you? You don't need to see them every time we come to market day." Or talk about them all the way home. He rolled his eyes. "How about I take you back to your mom and then you can go with Jan and the girls to see the rabbits?"

Jacob's eyes went wide, then watered. "But I want to stay with you."

Shoot. Not tears. Anything but the waterfall. "You can't go crying on me when you don't get your way, or else I'm leaving you with your mom for sure."

The boy ducked his head and swiped at his eyes. "I'm not crying."

Well, now he felt bad. *Ugh, kids.*

A tap on his shoulder pulled his attention from Jacob. Rob

stood behind him with a girl about Jan's age. "Hey, man. Good to see you." Rob gestured toward the girl. "This is my cousin, Olivia. She's staying with us until her dad finds a local place to live."

"Hi." Caleb nodded at the girl. "I'm Caleb."

Brilliant conversation starter there, dude. His brain seemed to slog in slow motion. Probably because Olivia had the longest, shiniest, and silkiest hair he'd ever seen. The brown locks trailed down her sides and back to just above her beltline. Her well-worn but clean jeans and T-shirt enhanced her petite form. Big brown eyes behind long, thick lashes beckoned him to smile. He couldn't stop smiling.

Her long, slim fingers reached out to him. What did she want? He flexed his empty hands as if searching for something to hand to her. *Oh! Shake her hand, dummy.* He reached out and shook the delicate appendage.

She returned the smile. "It's nice to meet you, Caleb. Rob has told me a few stories about you." The gorgeous smile moved away from him. "And who might this young man be?"

Right, he'd forgotten the boy was standing beside him. His brain froze. *What was the kid's name again?*

Not waiting for the delayed introduction, the boy cocked his head Olivia's way, his smile shy. "I'm Jacob."

She stooped to the boy's level and held her hand out for a shake, which Jacob accepted. "And it's a pleasure to meet you."

Rob punched Caleb's shoulder, a bit too hard for their normal greeting, then winked. "Want to come over tonight? I've got a new mason jar."

Caleb winced as a mental reminder of nausea hit. "Sorry, can't make it. Maybe next time."

Jacob cleared his throat and whispered to Olivia. "Do you

like rabbits?"

Her grin deepened. "Why, I love rabbits. Do you have one?"

The shy-guy look vanished, and he grabbed her hand, pulling her toward the market tables. "Oh yes. *And* I know where to find the rabbits here with the softest ears. Come on. I'll show you."

Caleb was never so grateful to have to deal with Jacob's obsession as he was now. He trailed the two with Rob jabbering in his ear about something. He couldn't clear his mind enough to know what the conversation was about, though, not with that long, brown silk curtain in front of him.

7

Chapter Seven

More people than usual crowded into the market today. Caleb and Rob dodged in and out of the crowds to keep up as Jacob zigzagged through the throng, intent on finding the rabbits. Olivia trailed behind him, laughing at the boy's intensity.

About fifty yards ahead, Jacob stopped and began jumping and waving. The rest of them caught up where the bunnies hopped in their pen under and around the sales table.

"I've got a white one and a gray one, but they have brown and black ones too." Jacob rattled off the facts in quick succession while he stooped to pick up the smallest charcoal-colored bunny, then turned to show it to Olivia. "Would you like to come to our farm to see my rabbits?"

She stroked the tiny animal's fur. "Of course, I would. Rob tells me your place isn't too far away from where we live."

Her brilliant smile almost stopped Caleb's heart. Not seductive or mischievous, but innocent and heartwarming. Too bad that smile wasn't just for him. "Walking distance really," he said. Ugh. He resisted slapping his forehead. What a

53

stupid thing to say. Wasn't everything within walking distance these days?

Rob scooped a second rabbit into his palm and held it to Olivia. She accepted the animal and brushed her cheek against its tiny body. Rob elbowed Caleb, winked, and whispered. "Girls love animals, dude."

The classic light bulb finally went on in his head. "We raise Angus on our farm. I bet you'd love to see the calves. We've got a few really cute new ones."

She tossed her brunette hair back over her shoulder to make eye contact. "Oh, I'd love to see the babies." Then she passed the bunny to Rob. "Can you take me over to see them this weekend?"

Rob's triumphant grin told Caleb he'd planned this. "I'd love to." He winked at Caleb again. "I'll bring refreshments as well. Just like a good Southern visitor should."

A voice cleared behind them. "Well now. Can I get in on that invite?"

Emma, hip cocked to the side, a smile revealing her perfectly white teeth, stood a few feet away. Curled tendrils of hair fluttered in the slight breeze, accentuating her blue eyes.

Caleb, stunned, swallowed hard against a throat that had gone dry. "Emma. Where did you come from?"

She stepped closer and reached to pet the bunny in Jacob's hands. "Oh, I wander around the market all the time. I saw you as I was passing through and thought I'd stop over to say hello." She nodded to Olivia and Rob. "And who might ya'll be? Friends of Caleb's?"

Right. He had obligations he was faltering on. "Emma, this is my neighbor, Rob, and his cousin, Olivia. She's new to the area."

"Welcome to our neck of the woods, Olivia." Emma's smile didn't reach her eyes until she stuck out her hand to Rob. "A pleasure to meet you, Rob. Surely I can get an invitation to the party?"

Rob stood tall, stretched to his full five-foot, eleven-inch height, and arched his back. "If I have anything to do with the invites, you'll be at the top of the list." He clicked his tongue, shoved his hands in his jeans pockets, and rocked back on his heels. "In fact, you might want to skip the cow fest and come right to the cookout at my house."

Caleb hadn't heard of anything going on at Rob's house. "A cookout?"

Emma sidled over and wrapped her arm through Caleb's, then grinned at Rob. "I'm assuming there won't be hotdogs and marshmallows?"

Rob's face fell. "Got me there. It's less of a cookout and more of a roast." He paused as if trying to build tension, but Emma and Olivia just waited. "You know—a pig roast. I'm sure we can hunt up a wild pig, right, buddy?"

Jacob's eyes went wide. "Pig hunting? Can I come?" He dropped the animal back into the bunny pen. "I can hunt too."

What was Rob thinking? Yes, there'd been wild pigs on the farm recently, but there was no guarantee they'd kill one on any specific day. The boar had only recently moved into the area. Caleb ruffled Jacob's hair. "We'll have to see, buddy."

But Olivia was eyeing Emma's claim on his arm, so he extracted himself from the hold. Not that Emma's touch wasn't pleasant. She was warm and soft against his side. But Olivia was beautiful as well. He barely knew Emma, after all. Best not to limit himself before he knew what these females were all about. He wanted these two ladies to be in his company for a while so he could get to know them better.

He spread out his hands. "Tell you what. Let's plan a hunt for this weekend. We'll go out Friday night hunting, and if it goes well, we'll have a pig to roast Saturday evening. How's that sound?"

Rob's face lit up as bright as Jacob's had. "Let's do it." Then he dipped his head to Emma's eye level, shaggy brown hair falling over his forehead. "Think you could make it out to my place if I give you the address?"

She flipped her hair and shifted her weight to her other foot, cocking her opposite hip. "I could make that happen." She flashed a wink at Rob, then a slow smile at Caleb. "I'll bring the party hats."

«»

"Kacie, no!" Caleb awoke, his heart pounding in his ears. The same nightmare had visited him on and off for three years. She was always standing on a stool, a rope around her neck and a tear on her cheek. He shook his head and swiped at his sweaty face, taking deep breaths to calm the racing in his chest.

Would she ever leave his dreams at peace? It was as if she were haunting him. He didn't believe in ghosts. But the mind had a way of tormenting the soul, and these nightmares seemed to be his venue of choice for processing the past.

It was always a long day when it started like this. If only he could release her memory and dwell on the happy recollections instead of the tragic end.

Refocus. Let it go, Caleb.

He scrubbed the dream from his focus, climbed out of bed, and headed for the shower. Today should be an interesting day.

«»

"Jacob, watch where you're stepping," Caleb growled. "We don't need your skinny butt falling through the floor into Jan's bedroom."

Jacob rolled his eyes and stepped to the next beam, kicking up dust as he followed Caleb and Mr. Jenkins through the attic. "I'm not stupid."

Mr. Jenkins let the measuring tape zip back into its place once more. He made a mental note of the additional dimensions. "And where did you plan to put your kitchenette?"

A sneeze twitching at his nostrils, Caleb moved closer to the attic entry hole where the steps descended. "On this side. I wanted to change the drop-down stairs into a dumbwaiter. It'll work since it's up against an outside wall."

Mr. Jenkins rubbed his rough palms across his scruffy gray-streaked beard, producing a scratching sound. "Should work, or you could put in a corkscrew staircase. Though I don't have a clue where you'd get one of those these days, and they're a pain to hand build."

Jacob jumped from one exposed beam to the next, near the end of the attic, as if playing hopscotch. More dust billowed. "Can I share your apartment with you, Caleb? There's room for two up here."

"You're about to get kicked out permanently if you don't stop hopping around." He'd maxed out on the boy's antics while he was trying to get serious work done. "Get out from back there. Now."

Okay, now he sounded like his father. All he needed to do was up the volume a smidge and he'd be a bellowing Worthington too. Maybe he didn't want kids after all.

Jacob's shoulders slumped as he inched his way back to the front of the attic.

Mr. Jenkins pulled his flask out of his paint-spattered overall pocket and spit tobacco juice. "I should have everything you need to fix this attic up. But it won't be cheap."

Caleb shoved his hands deep into his blue jeans pockets. He hated the setup for discussing prices. "Yes, sir. We established it would be costly."

The pause was almost painful to endure. There would be no speeding up the haggling process. Dad offered to help with the negotiations, but Caleb wanted the independence of doing this on his own. Still, he should've allowed Dad to be here as a reinforcement.

Mr. Jenkins continued inspecting the room as if he weren't sure what all they needed for the job. *If he doesn't say something soon, I'm going to explode.*

"I like steaks," Mr. Jenkins said. "Haven't eaten but one or two rib eyes since everything fell apart with the big variant wave in '22. I'd like to taste them again. Regularly."

The silence after that statement caused so many questions to run through Caleb's head that it was almost deafening. What did that mean? Was he asking for a lifetime supply or what? *Best not to say too much.* "Yes, sir. I can appreciate that thought."

That was a generic enough response, wasn't it?

All fidgeting with tools and wandering eyes ceased. Mr. Jenkins's full attention landed on Caleb's face. Seeing every line stressing Mr. Jenkins's eyes, Caleb felt as if he was measuring him as a man.

A loud thump distracted them. They pivoted as Jacob popped up out of the box he'd tripped over and fallen into. "I'm okay."

Caleb glared at the youngster, who then started for the pull-down staircase.

Jacob blushed. "I'm going downstairs to see what Mom's doing."

"Good idea." Caleb returned his attention to Mr. Jenkins.

"I'd like fourteen rib eye steaks per week for the next year. Deliverable on market day each week. Good quality, no skinny cows you're trying to get rid of. I want marbling that'll sizzle on the grill."

A dreamy look glazed the man's eyes as if he had a juicy steak in front of him after a week of fasting.

That was a lot of steaks. Over seven hundred of them. One cow produced less than thirty rib eyes. It would take almost thirty cows to produce all the cuts he was asking for—not going to happen. This was just the beginning of the negotiation, and Caleb wouldn't capitulate. *Let the games begin.*

He twisted his mouth to the side and furrowed his brow as if deep in thought. "Now, you know I can't butcher half our herd for your dinner." Direct eye contact was critical here. Time to look him square in the eye. "But we can provide you an excellent steak dinner for your Sunday meals. That's what you're really after, anyway."

Mr. Jenkins frowned and spit into his flask.

Caleb continued. "When's the last time you had a filet mignon? You know what I mean? So tender you can cut it with a butter knife, and juicy because the marbling is perfect."

He swore a bit of drool escaped the corner of Mr. Jenkins's lips, and it wasn't from the chaw in his cheek. "Hmm. Those are good, but too small. I need a man-sized hunk of meat."

Counter negotiations were all a part of the challenge. It didn't fool him into thinking his opponent didn't want the choice cuts. "Tell you what. I'm going to offer you two packages of filet mignon today—*before* you even deliver a single wallboard screw. You'll be dining high on the hog tonight, because I'm going to add some potatoes, and Mom's famous canned beans, perfectly salted, to the mix."

The flask came back out with a double spit. "Yeah? What else? I'm no fool to give away that much for one meal."

"Oh, that's only the beginning, just to whet your appetite." He winked, hoping it wasn't too dramatic. "We're going to meet up every week at the auction, and I'm going to hand over those two rib eye steaks for your Sunday dinner, a roast for your midweek hump that'll provide leftovers for lunch the next day, and five pounds of hamburger. That means beef, every night of the week for an entire year."

Spitting and silence were his answer. Mr. Jenkins stared at the ground, rubbed his head, then massaged the back of his neck. When he spoke, it came out rapid fire. "Hamburger? You want me to give you something as hard to find as wallboard for *hamburger*? You can do better than that."

It was Caleb's turn to think and let his opponent wait in silence. Each of his steers would produce about four hundred and thirty pounds of beef in its various forms. To spread the amount over a year would be no problem, but most of it would be ground beef, roasts, or stew—not steak.

Bring it home, dude. Bring it home.

"Come now. You know most people are lucky to get beef once a month. You'll be so sick of beef you'll be trading some of that burger for someone's chicken or fish before fall hits." He stuck his hand out toward Mr. Jenkins. "I'll swap one of those pounds of burger out for stew meat each week. Deal?"

Mr. Jenkins hung his head, focused on his feet, pushing a bit of insulation around with his left toe. Another spit. Then his head popped up, and he grabbed Caleb's hand with his enormous paw. "Deal."

8

Chapter Eight

Caleb swore the ruts would swallow the truck as it bumped down the dirt farm road. Dad avoided the worst of it. A low moan emanated from the back seat, and the rearview mirror captured Rob, pale as paste. His friend wasn't prone to motion sickness, so what was up? "You okay?"

Rob rolled his window down and stuck his nose outside the truck. "Swell."

It had been a long time since they'd taken Rob hunting. Perhaps he was nervous about shooting the rifle again, but he'd been acting weird all evening. Normally, Rob would've been joking with his sister and tossing fake punches at Jacob, goofing around. Not this evening, though. Something was on his mind.

Rob wasn't the only person out of sorts tonight. Jacob had wailed when Dad told him he couldn't come. "It's not fair. I don't get to go anywhere with you guys. I want to hunt too."

Caleb was twelve years old when Dad first took him hunting. The shotgun's recoil slamming into his shoulder with his first shot was a permanent memory.

Dad didn't put up with the younger boy carrying on. "We've already discussed this. If you don't stop complaining, you might not see a gun until you're ninety."

Thankfully, Mrs. Dunwoody collected Jacob and said she'd play a game with him. He'd pouted until they'd left.

Unwilling to make frivolous trips, they didn't often take the truck anyplace except on auction day, but pig hunting required the enormous truck bed. They couldn't haul an oversized wild pig in the back of a golf cart. Hopefully, they'd bag more than one of the immense beasts.

The best place to find a wild pig was around a peanut farm, and the closest one was south of Shiloh, in Taylor County. An old friend of Dad's allowed them to hunt the property whenever they wanted. Feral swine had been an issue in Georgia before COVID struck in 2020. The depopulation of humans in 2022 allowed the herds to explode. With the southernmost Georgia farms so covered in the animals, farming crops was difficult. This homestead wasn't quite that badly off, but the open invitation remained.

About an hour before sunset, they arrived at the wide-open field planted with acres of peanuts, an impressive crop size. Few farmers could afford the fuel the massive planters used. Smaller planters existed, but it took a lot of man-hours to run them. The field's owner had figured out a method, as the huge planting was all uniform rows.

They followed a trail they'd previously used and trooped along the edge of the wood line surrounding the area. Dad led them. Rob lagged like a three-year-old who didn't want to go to the barber.

They stopped at an old deer stand in the far corner. It had

a rusted but solid set of rungs. While the contraption was freestanding, it backed up to a giant oak tree. Dad signaled for them to look up the trail. Downwind and northwest of the stand stood a burlap-wrapped tree the farmer maintained.

Back when oil changes were commonplace, they used motor oil to soak the burlap around the tree. Pigs rubbed up against the burlap to keep flies off them. The perfect lure brought the hunter's prey in close. A well-worn pig trail circled the tree. The gunny didn't appear to have fresh oil, but the old habits were still in play.

A rope they'd brought along hung around Dad's shoulder. He adjusted it after handing Caleb his rifle, preparing for the climb. As per their plan, Dad signaled to Rob, pointing first to his gun, then to the bucket he held.

Rob nodded and handed his gun to Caleb, then took the five-gallon bucket and walked along the edge of the field, scattering the corn between the stand and the burlap tree. Rob couldn't seem to stay on the path. He veered into the field and the scrub on opposite sides of the game trail. What was up with him tonight?

They'd only filled the bucket half-full, so it didn't take long to distribute the entire contents around the area. Once he finished, Rob returned to the tree.

Dad dropped the rope end down from the stand. He never climbed a tree with a loaded gun. They always carried the long rope so the first person up the ladder would haul up any weapons or other items they brought for the hunt.

Caleb tied Dad's rifle to the end of the line, and Dad hoisted it onto the stand. Once he'd safeguarded the rifle above, the rope dropped again, and they repeated the process with Caleb's and Rob's rifles.

Then Caleb motioned to Rob after Dad secured the guns. With his friend acting weird, leaving him on the ground alone didn't feel right. As Rob moved past him, Caleb glimpsed his unfocused eyes.

What was going on? Was Rob sick and didn't want to tell them? They both wanted that pig to roast this weekend, but if Rob was sick, they wouldn't end up having a party, anyway.

His friend's struggle up the ladder was almost painful to watch. Caleb ground his teeth. If he'd realized earlier Rob was out of sorts, he'd have canceled the hunt. If Rob fell out of the stand, Caleb would never forgive himself. He almost hollered to his dad they needed to go home, but then Rob hit the top rung and climbed onto the platform. Well, he was up. Better let him rest before they dragged him back down.

The platform towered twelve feet above the field. Three could stand on it, but there were only two seats. While they knew it would be tight, Dad insisted he join them since wild boars could be dangerous. Caleb sat on the seat opposite his friend while Dad wound the rope around the tree, then attached a hook to the rope on one end and his belt on the other.

Caleb attached a hook to his own belt, connecting himself to the stand. Rob hadn't yet mimicked the action, so Caleb nudged his father's thigh and pointed to the dangling safety rope on Rob's chair. Dad shook his head, then smacked the back of Rob's head. His drooping head shot up with the blow. When Dad used quick hand signals to point out the forgotten safety device, Rob attached himself.

Satisfied Rob was secure, Caleb and Dad faced the burlap tree. The scuffles of animals in the surrounding woods were a treat to the ears. This part of the quest invigorated him—listening for the grunt of incoming pigs opened his senses up to hear a myriad of woodland creatures. The rustling leaves nearby revealed a squirrel running across the limbs. A turkey gobbled in the distance, too far away for them to have a chance of spotting it.

The setting sun illuminated the clouds with orange, red, and golden flight paths for the bats swooping for insects. If he could've captured this moment of breathtaking view, he'd turn it into a picture for his apartment walls. Perhaps he was just as wild a creature as those surrounding him.

A grunt came from behind the burlap tree. Peeking sideways, he saw Dad alerted to the sound as well. Rob appeared to have fallen asleep. Seriously?

More grunting sounds, followed by squeals, heralded a herd headed toward them. The various intonations implied a sow with piglets at a minimum, probably a few older females and males as well. They raised their rifles and aimed toward the tree. Dad's foot slid over and tapped Caleb's toes. The signal to be ready. They'd practiced this stance for years to maximize their harvest by synchronizing their shots.

The first piglet came around the tree, rubbing its snout on the burlap. The sow followed, surrounded by the rest of her litter. A few older gilts and barrows, most likely from her prior litter, accompanied her as well. It was a good-sized crowd—more than a dozen animals. Caleb aimed for the sow. Dad would allow him the biggest target, as was their tradition.

One tap against his toes, two taps. With the third tap, they both fired. Two of the pigs dropped to the ground, the sow and the larger of her offspring. While the sow appeared to be dead, the yearling squealed in pain. The herd scattered with the shots but ran back again to the squealer. They both shot again and dropped two more.

Rob jumped to his feet, awakened. He brought his rifle up, but he struggled to steady the gun. When it wavered in his hands, Dad reached over and pushed the barrel down and away, then shook his head at Rob. After a moment's hesitation, Rob lowered his weapon and sat back down.

Dad aimed and shot once more at the dying pig, ending its struggle. This restored calm into the woods as the snorting and grunting herd retreated. Dad lowered his rifle and scowled at Rob. "Son, what is the matter with you? Your aim was as wobbly as a newborn calf trying to nurse for the first time."

"Sorry, Mr. Worthington." Rob shrugged. "I guess I'm exhausted."

Dad extracted the gun from Rob's lap. "If you're too tired to hunt, then you should've stayed home. This isn't a game. You could have shot one of us—or even yourself."

Rob dropped his head in a quick bob. "Yes, sir. Sorry, sir."

Rob had been hunting with them too many times to make stupid mistakes. So what was going on with him?

"Good shot, son." Dad leaned both his and Rob's guns against the tree trunk. "I'd say we're going to have one fancy pig roast with one of those yearlings."

"Yes, sir." Caleb couldn't contain his grin. "We'll be inviting all the neighbors to this shindig."

Dad sucked in a deep breath of the evening air, satisfaction smoothing the lines on his work-hardened face. "Let's get down and dress those pigs before it's too dark. It's a way back to the truck, and you've got a mighty big carcass to drag. Whoever shoots the big one drags the big one."

They reversed their safety protocol to retreat down the ladder. Caleb handed his weapon off to Dad and scrambled down the ladder. When he reached the bottom, Caleb grasped the ladder as Rob maneuvered a foot into position on the top rung.

His heart lurched into his throat when Rob missed the second rung and collapsed against the rails, hands white with the exertion of holding on without a foothold. Dad grabbed the collar of Rob's shirt to steady him until he regained his foothold. The slow crawl to the bottom seemed to last a lifetime.

Rob's last step to the ground was unsteady.

Caleb had to know what was going on with his friend. As soon as Rob was solid on his feet, he grabbed his shoulder and spun Rob around to face him. "Dude, what is your problem tonight?" A slow burn started in his brain. "Have you been drinking?"

Rob's face flushed red. "Shh. Your dad'll hear." His friend pulled a flask out of his hip pocket. "Just a nip. You know. To take the edge off."

As the burn in Caleb's head burst into a roaring blaze, he barely maintained a whisper. "Have you lost your mind? You're drinking and carrying a loaded weapon? You could have killed one of us." He punched his friend on the arm—hard. "Maybe even yourself, doofus."

"Hey, pay attention," Dad bellowed from above. "Weapons descending." He pointed to a patch of grass in the moonlight. "Move your happy butt away from the ladder and stand over there, out of the way."

After the first gun touched the ground, Caleb untied it from the rope, then yelled to his father to send the next one down. Once the weapons were all at ground level, Dad joined them.

"Time to dress some pigs, gentlemen." Dad wound the rope

into large loops, secured it over his shoulder, then retrieved his rifle.

Caleb collected both remaining rifles and walked to the path. Dad's quizzical stare pointed at the rifles. Caleb just shook his head once. "Rob's gonna haul the bigger pig and let me take two smaller ones. The least I can do for him is carry his gun."

If he got lucky, the explanation might suffice and not encourage additional questions. Dad shrugged and moved to the pigs to begin field dressing.

Rob followed and whispered, "Thanks for not ratting me out, man."

With his anger so white-hot, Caleb couldn't even look back at the idiot. "You owe me, big time."

They worked for the next hour getting the carcasses ready for transport and then hauled them to the truck.

Was Rob turning into an alcoholic?

9

Chapter Nine

It seemed like forever since they'd had a pig roast, and this was the largest group of neighbors Caleb had seen in a while. All afternoon, Jan and her friends, Lizzy and Renee, had been giggling and carrying on. He'd barely been able to get enough time in the bathroom to shower. The girls primped for hours to make their hair do what nature never intended.

Just why did women always want the opposite of what they had? If their hair was curly, they wanted it straight. If it was straight, of course, they wanted it curly. He'd never tell Jan, but his sister was beautiful the way she was. Her BFF, Renee, had grown to be a beauty as well. Lizzy was cute too, but man, could she talk. She. Never. Shut. Up.

He'd have sworn Renee had been flirting with him a few times today, but he'd always thought of her as a sister.

The smallest of the pigs had been at least fifty pounds after they dressed it, and it would be the center of attention tonight. They turned it on a spit over the roaring fire Rob and his dad had built.

Berry pie, cornbread, roasted potatoes, and green beans would accompany the pig once they'd roasted it. He'd helped the men set up the spit earlier in the day, setting the metal bars they'd pulled from storage in the garage into place. They'd left the Jacksons to build and tend the fire, then returned home to finish evening chores and prepare the rest of the food for the party.

Now they gathered as friends. The Worthingtons, Boswells, Dunwoodys, Jacksons, and Tilbrooks represented their small but growing neighborhood. The setting sun, burning orange on the horizon, enhanced the celebratory mood.

Lizzy had helped Jacob catch fireflies in a mason jar, and the glowing container flickered and flashed with its occupants' communications. Jacob made sure everyone knew about the container and his adventures in capturing the bugs, though Caleb suspected Lizzy caught many of them, as Jacob struggled to snag the insects without smashing them. He'd learn.

When Rob arrived, he offered a nip out of his flask, "just to liven things up a bit," but Caleb refused. He had no desire for a repeat of the morning-after-moonshine event, but that didn't seem to stop Rob. Where was he getting this stuff, anyway?

Logs surrounded the fire pit, acting as seating. Blankets kept the tree bark from digging into their pant legs. Sparks flew into the air, accompanied by loud pops from the fire while savory scents of roasting pig promised it was close to done.

The stars sparkled above the wood line as the full moon lit up the front yard. He sat on the edge of one log, Rob on his left, and Olivia on Rob's left. Caleb laughed at a goofy face Olivia made at Jacob, teasing him about squashing too many fireflies. Laughter felt good, and somehow, her laughter soothed his soul. She glistened with the moonlight and firelight reflections dancing in her hair. He could've sat all night, watching and listening.

A hand grasped his shoulder—huh, Emma stood behind him. In his surprise, his voice jumped an octave. "Where did you come from?"

Her even white teeth glowed. "Well, hello to you too. You invited me, remember?"

Her slim hip cocked to the side with her small hand rested on it. She flicked her curls back and winked at him, then at Rob. "Is there room for one more on that log?"

Rob scooted over, pushing Olivia to the edge, and patted the area between himself and Caleb. "Always room for you, my dear."

Caleb narrowed his eyes. If Rob had pushed any harder, he'd have knocked Olivia to the ground. She may be Rob's cousin, but tossing her around like a rag doll still wasn't appropriate.

Before Caleb could voice his displeasure, Emma hopped onto the log, wiggling her hips as if to make room between himself and Rob, as if there weren't plenty of space already. She placed a hand on each of their arms. "The cooking smells heavenly. Do you folks eat like this all the time? They've rationed most folks around here pretty thinly these days."

Rob sprang on the question like a starving flea on a passing mutt. "We hunted up some pigs south of here, just for tonight." What a dopey smile. "Had to be sure you'd have a good meal if you made a special trip, didn't we?"

Emma rubbed her shoulder up against Rob's. "Well, aren't you a sweet gentleman?" Then, tipping her face toward Caleb, she winked her long lashes. "And you? Do you eat high on the hog, so to speak, regularly?"

Man, who could resist staring into her eyes? They were

mesmerizing. "Not really. It takes gas to travel down to where the pigs are, so we don't go often." He inhaled her scent, and though he couldn't figure out what she smelled like, it was heavenly. "So, when we go, we try to bag as many as we can."

Her lips rose. Too bad, he couldn't bottle that slow smile up and take it home to enjoy later.

A jab to his shoulder yanked his attention from Emma. "Hey." Jacob stood in front of him, a frown cemented on his lips.

"I've been talking, and you've been ignoring me." His no longer noodle-thin arms crossed over his chest as he copped a no-nonsense stance. "You said you'd help catch fireflies, remember?"

He had? Oh yeah. Olivia had. Olivia promised to help catch some more bugs, and Caleb was supposed to go with them. Emma's presence seemed to command all his attention whenever she was around—like some sort of hypnotism or something. "Sure, buddy. Sorry about that. You ready to go?"

The frown transformed, and Jacob dashed to the opposite end of the log. He pulled Olivia to her feet, then beckoned Caleb. "Let's go."

They headed out to the backyard where the fireflies lit up like party lights someone had scattered for the event. Back at the log, Rob sneaked his flask to Emma. She took a pull at it. Apparently, she was up for the party Rob ached for. Good for them. Maybe they'd be happy together and not sick as dogs tomorrow.

She wasn't Caleb's type, anyway. Just because her curly blond hair bounced as she walked and he could get lost in those blue eyes didn't mean she was the right one for him.

Maybe she was humoring Rob, sipping his moonshine to fit in and she wasn't really a party girl. He'd have to think on that one later.

"Pay attention, Caleb." Jacob shoved a jar into Caleb's hands. "You're missing all the fireflies in front of you."

Olivia snickered. "Caleb has something on his mind besides bugs right now, Jacob. Maybe you should let him go back with Rob and Emma."

"Sorry, buddy." His face flushed hot. Grasping the jar in his right hand, Caleb refocused. "You're going to have to show me how to catch them again. It's been a long time since I've done this."

Jacob went into excruciating detail on fireflies, how to catch them, why they lit up, and everything about the insects. As the boy rambled, Caleb focused on Olivia.

She'd pulled her hair back and spun it into a bun at the back of her head as they'd walked to the hunting area. Even tied up, it shone in the moonlight. A firefly landed on her head as she kneeled in the grass. Its light was as if an angel had descended on her and was trying to light a path to her for him. *Dude, you're losing it.*

How could he start a conversation with someone he knew nothing about? His heartbeat skittered as she held her hands out to him, a firefly cradled in the center for him to scoop into his jar. "Don't let Jacob drive you nuts. He'll talk about bugs all night, unless you ask him about his rabbits, then get ready for a truly boring evening."

Laughter lit her eyes like mini firelights flitted in them. "He's adorable. You don't know how lonely being an only child is, especially once your parents aren't around. Enjoy his enthusiasm while you can."

While Emma's blue eyes reminded him of the sky, Olivia's brown peepers prompted thoughts of his mother's tigereye ring—flecks of gold catching his attention. But was that sadness behind the laughter? "What happened to your parents?"

There, he'd done it now. All the laughter vanished from her eyes, and they blinked before she ducked her head. "Mom died in '22, along with her sister. We'd been at a party, and everyone there got sick." She swiped at a tear with the back of her hand, then reached for another lightning bug. "Dad and I recovered. Mom didn't. It hasn't been good since then. Dad drinks too much and doesn't work enough. When Uncle Kevin, Aunt Amanda, and Rob moved in with us, I thought Dad would stop drinking and get back to work."

When Rob and his family moved to Columbus to live with Olivia and her dad, they'd been so hopeful they'd find work in the city. They'd returned just as empty-handed as they'd left. "What brought you here to live with Rob's family?"

She walked her latest captured specimen over to him. As he slid his hand off the top of the jar, she deposited the bug. "After Rob's family left us, Dad didn't feel a need to hide his drinking anymore. It got worse. He'd lost his job already, but then he stopped even trying to pretend to find work. We lost our apartment. Crummy as it was, at least we had four walls and a roof. Being homeless isn't easy."

His heart dropped into his stomach, churning with the thought of her being homeless in Columbus. The marauders who attacked the farm earlier this year had come out of the larger city because Columbus had been so picked over. If even the bad guys didn't want to live there, it offered no haven for a teenage girl, especially if she couldn't trust her father to protect her.

After replacing his hand over the jar's mouth, he tipped it

upside down on a nearby rock. The fireflies lit up as if someone had inserted a string of twinkle lights. "How'd you end up here?"

She eyed the container, then tilted her face toward the stars. With light pollution no longer an issue, the stars seemed within an arm's reach. "Dad got mugged our first night on the street. I'd been waiting for him to come back to our tent in a wooded area by the highway. He planned to search the dumpsters for food." A faraway look glazed her eyes as if she'd left her body and returned to the past. "He didn't come back until the next morning, bloodied and bruised. Shortly after that, he decided it wasn't safe for me in the big city anymore. He brought me to my uncle's house until he can find work. I doubt he'll even look, though."

As his heart ached, he was grateful she didn't see him swipe at his eyes. Now wasn't the time to blubber like a girl. She needed him to be strong. "I'm glad you're here now. I'm sure your dad will figure things out now that he's on his own and has time to think."

Her head tipped his way. A wisp of escaped hair floated alongside her soft mouth as it curved into a smile—a smile that didn't lighten her eyes. "I hope so."

"Caleb." Jacob sprinted toward them, leaping over a fallen branch in his path while carrying his jar full of lightning bugs. "I'm starving. When are we going to eat?"

Caleb couldn't help but chuckle. Was Jacob ever *not* hungry? "Let's go check it out, buddy."

Jacob set his jar beside Caleb's, then grabbed Olivia's hand. "Caleb shot the pig himself. Did he tell you that?"

Now Olivia's smile reached her eyes, and the twinkle of playfulness was a bonus. She winked at him as Jacob dragged her toward the roasting spit. "Really?" she asked Jacob. "I thought for sure you'd been the one to track down our supper."

Jacob's face fell as he glared back at Caleb. Then the kid kicked at a loose stone along their way. "Oh no. I'm not old enough yet. Mr. Worthington said I can shoot when I'm twelve."

With no time for discussing hunting, they arrived right before Dad bellowed, "Attention, folks, our roast is ready. Gather 'round."

They all collected around the spit where the pig sizzled over the fire. Mom took over as soon as the group quieted down. "Let's bow our heads in thanks for the meal and for our friends to share it."

Clasping hands, they listened as Mom prayed. "Father, we're so grateful to be together to celebrate friendships...."

As Mom prayed, Caleb couldn't shake Olivia's story. He couldn't imagine losing his family. What if his mother had never recovered? She was still weak from her bout with the variant, but he still had her as well as his father and sister.

He'd have to make Rob clean up his act and be the family Olivia needed. Rob—Emma. As all chorused amen, he saw neither of them. Just great. What were they up to?

10

Chapter Ten

A buzz of conversation in the kitchen below drifted upward when Caleb awoke the next morning. Had he slept past breakfast? Wait a minute, better question—Was the entire neighborhood in their kitchen? Perhaps he'd missed a critical conversation last night. He racked his brain for what he'd forgotten.

They were supposed to be working out in the garden today, harvesting cabbage. He'd planned to get his share of the gardening knocked out quickly since Mr. Jenkins promised to drop off the building supplies today.

Caleb flicked a finger against the familiar field day trophy on his dresser, then pulled fresh jeans out of a drawer and slid them on. Fresh socks and a T-shirt completed the ensemble. He trundled down the stairs, ready for whatever awaited him.

When he stepped into the living room, the men were already eating in the dining room. Mr. Tilbrook, Mr. Boswell, and Mr. Jackson sat at the table as well. A full house indeed. Jacob occupied the table's far end, no plate in front of him, eyes staring at the tabletop. Something was up with that. The boy never sat quietly, nor did you see him not eating when others were. Caleb approached the boy, nodding to the other guests as he passed by. "What's up, buddy? Not hungry this morning?"

Head still dipped toward the table, Jacob fidgeted in the wicker chair Caleb's mom usually claimed. "Mom said I can't go to the garden with everyone today."

Odd. Mrs. Dunwoody worked as hard as the rest of the family and always brought Jacob along. "Why not?"

The boy blinked up at Caleb, his eyes glassy and red. "She said I can't go if I don't eat my breakfast, but I'm not hungry. My stomach feels weird."

Something was wrong if Jacob didn't eat. That explained why his mother banned him from the heat of garden work. "I can get you some eggs. I'm headed to the kitchen for my food."

With a shake of his head, Jacob crossed his arms on the table and laid his head on them. "I'm just gonna rest for a minute, so I'm ready to help when you bring the cabbages in. Mom said we're making sauerkraut."

Definitely something wrong. Caleb ruffled the boy's hair, then proceeded to the kitchen. All the conversations going on at once in the small area deafened him. How in the world could they understand each other amid the ruckus?

"Morning, Caleb." Renee scooted to his side, hands clasped behind her, slinky blond ponytail swinging. "Can I get you a plate?"

She was always so friendly, like a younger sister, except she wanted to do stuff for him—a sweet kid, for sure. "Thanks, I got it."

The egg pan was close to empty already, but he scooped out the remaining scrambled goodness and the last of the potatoes from their skillet. Mom was going to try making ketchup this year. The experiment better go well because he sure missed the condiment on mornings like this.

Mom gave him a side hug as he headed toward the dining room. "Morning. I hope we didn't wake you. Everyone was excited to get the food pantry started today and showed up early." She pointed to his meager breakfast. "I can make some more. I didn't expect everyone to arrive hungry."

He kissed her cheek. She'd bend over backward to ensure her children had all they needed, even if she wasn't feeling up to it. "This is fine."

Then his chest tightened as he frowned at Mrs. Dunwoody. "Is Jacob okay? He didn't want to eat?"

She waved him off. "Morning, Caleb. I'm not sure what's going on with him. Something isn't right, though. He's not prone to tummy aches, but perhaps the cookout didn't agree with him. I'm keeping him inside today, just to be sure."

"Morning, big brother." Jan danced over like she'd been cheering at a football game and didn't want to lose her pep. "We're canning extra today to add to the food pantry. Word is getting around at the market that we're starting soon, and some of the bigger merchants will pitch in. Isn't it exciting?"

Seeing her enthused about a new project always cheered him up. Having friendships back in her life after this past year of solitude perked her up like water on a wilting plant. She'd be antsy to hand out the first food gifts.

After they finished eating, they headed out as a group to the garden where the cabbages were ripening. Now that they had so many people to help and feed, the garden had grown tremendously. All the work was manual. Planting, weeding, watering, and harvesting took *hours*. What had been a reasonable plot of food for a family of four now sprawled over five acres and promised to feed all of them, plus offer a bounty to sell or share.

His job usually involved lifting. After the ladies cut the cabbages and placed them into half-bushel baskets, the men would gather them onto the golf cart until only the driver and a helper standing on the back would fit. Then the two would drive the baskets back to the house to unload.

They filled three carts with produce by the end of the morning. Then all filed back to the house to eat a quick lunch of the pinto beans and cornbread Mom and Mrs. Dunwoody prepared.

Caleb's stomach growled at the savory smell, but he didn't see Jacob. His chest and legs felt as though weighed down with body armor as he sidled up to Mrs. Dunwoody. "Where's my buddy?"

"He fell asleep on the couch not long after everyone left, so I took him back to his bed to rest." She eyed the ceiling as if she could see the boy through it. "I'll admit I'm worried. It takes a lot to keep him from the action."

He'd need to check on the boy after lunch. It had been a while since someone in the house had been sick. Uneasy prickles crept across his chest, and he shuddered, remembering when the entire family had come down with the variant. They'd hospitalized Mom for a month before she'd returned home. She remained in a weakened state to this day. Perhaps their group of friends had grown too large. Was it possible the variant could make a comeback?

He joined the line to gather his scoop of beans and slab of cornbread, but he couldn't shake this… unease. After he seated himself, Mom asked for a blessing on the food before everyone dug in. He added a silent prayer for his little buddy.

As he crumbled his cornbread into his beans, talk around the table broke into multiple smaller conversations. He struggled to concentrate. So he wolfed down the food to avoid remaining in the raucous environment.

When a knock at the door rescued him, he popped out of his chair and hustled to answer it.

Dressed in blue jean coveralls and a paint-spattered T-shirt, Mr. Jenkins leaned to spit over the handrail, then nodded to Caleb. "Afternoon. You ready to get started on that remodel? 'Cause I'm ready to eat some beef tonight."

"Born ready. Let's get it unloaded." He hollered toward the dining room. "We could use some help to unload, gentlemen."

The men gathered around the flatbed trailer filled to the point of overload. Some items hadn't been available for a long time, so they ogled the contents of the steel contraption on wheels. Strapped together in a heap were insulation rolls, along with wallboard, joint compound, wallboard screws, four-by-fours, and nails. Mr. Jenkins's assistant exited the truck's passenger side and pulled a five-gallon bucket from the back seat, bringing it around and setting it at Caleb's feet.

Caleb bent to read the label, then jerked his head up. "Paint primer? I'd forgotten that even existed. How'd you get it?"

"Unfortunately, primer will have to do for now." The shaggy-haired assistant straightened his paint-splattered coveralls, then held his hand out to shake. "Sold the last of the paint this past fall. I'm John Jenkins. Nice to meet you."

Caleb accepted the proffered greeting and shook with vigor. "It's great to meet you, John. I'm ready to get this project going. Let's unload her."

As the Jenkins team unfastened the straps holding the load in place, a line formed to pick up and haul the various materials into the house and up the stairs to the attic. It got tricky once the wallboard was ready to be moved up the final set of stairs.

With the opening a smidgen too small to allow the materials to pass through, Dad looked back and forth between the wallboard lined up in the hallway and the opening attic. "Well, son, you've got your first decision to make. Are we cutting the wallboard down to get it up the stairs? Or are we widening the opening?"

Good question. Caleb rocked back and forth on his heels. "If we cut the wallboard down, then it is extra work to fill in and sand all those seams. But if we cut the opening wider, we'll have extra work to make it look good again from down here."

Mr. Jenkins walked up behind them. "You were planning a dumbwaiter to get upstairs. I'm assuming you've already got the pulleys?"

"Yes, sir. Found some at one of the market booths. That's what gave me the idea."

"Then you might as well get the opening widened for your dumbwaiter now. Just use a platform at first so you can get your materials up there. Then you can enclose it when you're all finished." He fished out his flask, unscrewed the lid, and spit into it. "Just don't forget the furniture before you enclose it. Or you could even leave it semi-open for changing things out in the future. The women in our lives always seem to change things, anyway."

"Excellent idea!" Caleb did a fist pump. "I'll make that my first project. Until then, we'll have to deal with a hallway full of wallboard."

He climbed up the stairs one last time to take up a bucket of joint compound. They'd moved boxes stored for years to one corner, over top a sheet of plywood. Eventually, they'd need to be sorted and discarded or stored elsewhere. Invigorated by the stack of building materials, he envisioned the finished room. His own place where he could be alone if he wanted—or even bring his first date.

He'd better learn how to cook soon, or he'd never be independent. Food. That reminded him. Clambering back down the steps, he rejoined Dad and Mr. Jenkins, who were still discussing the optimal way to widen the attic opening. "I owe you the first week of beef, sir."

A broad smile crinkled up on Mr. Jenkins's face, revealing tobacco specks stuck between his teeth. "I believe you do, son."

11

Chapter Eleven

The frozen hamburger meat packages didn't want to stack neatly, so Caleb gave up the effort at tidiness and shoved the one-pound bundles on top of two rib eye steaks, a roast, and a package of stew beef.

In the week since Mr. Jenkins dropped off the supplies, Caleb had framed out new walls so he could tell where his bedroom would be in relation to his sitting area, kitchenette, and tiny dining room. The apartment wouldn't be palatial, but it would be *his*. Once he completed it, the next project would be a staircase to the outside, so he wouldn't have to go through the house unless he wanted to.

Hefting the bushel basket to his shoulder, he headed to the golf cart they'd loaded for market day. With no cattle to sell today, they wouldn't take the truck. That limited who could come this week. Since he had a delivery to make, he'd serve as male protection and had tucked a sidearm under his shirt, just in case.

As he passed the kitchen, Mrs. Dunwoody spoke to Mom in subdued tones through the mask she wore. "I don't think he's getting any worse, but he doesn't seem to get better either."

Jacob—he'd started running a fever the evening they'd harvested cabbage. He hadn't been out of his room since. It had to be quite a bug to keep that kid in bed. Man, how Caleb missed the days when they could've driven Jacob to the doctor or popped into an urgent care to see what was wrong. Even the local hospital had closed when they ran out of nurses. Few of them wanted to work through the pandemic. Who could blame them with all the political shenanigans and people up in arms on both sides of the vaccine debate?

Caleb set the basket on the marble counter. "Do you think it's time to take him to Doc?"

The local vet had helped before with Jacob. They only used Doc's services in extreme cases, but since the boy had been sick for an entire week, this might be a good time.

"It may be." Mom sighed, then crossed her arms over her chest. "What do you think, Megan?"

Mrs. Dunwoody shrugged, twisting and untwisting the towel in her hands. "Since he can't run tests, Doc would just tell us to treat the fever, like we have been. I don't want to expose more people than necessary. Who knows? He might have the variant. It's been a while since we've seen a case, but the population in the area is growing. It might be."

She'd kept Jacob away from the family and wore her mask. It reminded Caleb of the time before the schools had permanently closed. He'd hated those face-smothering coverings.

Mom rubbed Mrs. Dunwoody's back as if to comfort the comforter. "He's young. He'll spring back soon, I'm sure." Then she raised a brow at Caleb. "You ready to go? Time's a-wastin.'"

He hefted the basket onto his shoulder once more. "Yes,

ma'am. This was the last I needed."

"The girls are joining us today to help with the table." Mom shooed him along. "Jan is excited about drumming up more contributors for the food pantry."

Great. Another trip with a loaded-down cart full of giggling girls. At what age did girls turn into women and stop being so silly? Such was the life of an older brother. "I'll meet you outside."

As he tromped to the carport door, Jan, Lizzy, Renee, and Mrs. Boswell stood waiting and, of course, laughing. When he stepped outside, Renee's head swiveled toward him. "Morning, Caleb. Can I help with that?"

She scooted over to him as he set the basket in the third-row seat, adding to the heap of goods. Today was more about being a mobile food pantry than about selling, but they had some items for sale, including his projects. With only room for one person to sit in the third row, even then, whoever got stuck here would hold at least one basket, their feet propped on another. "Thanks. I've got it."

Her smile drooped, her suntanned cheeks sagging. "Just let me know what I can do to help. I could watch your whittling for you at the table today."

Such a sweet kid, always willing to help him. "I appreciate the offer. I've got some business to take care of first thing. If you could watch my stuff so Mom doesn't have to do it all, that'd be great."

She popped up on her toes, then rocked back on her heels. "Sure thing."

Mom exited with one last basket of dried beef. The jerky sold well since few had consistent electricity to power refrigeration. Some would can their meat, but others preferred dehydrated because more of it fit into a jar for storage. She claimed the shotgun seat, then patted his arm. "Let's go, team."

The long drive in the cart was less painful than expected. With plenty to think about, he brooded most of the way. Visions of his apartment project, Emma, Olivia, and even Kacie bombarded him, refusing to give him peace.

After helping unload the cart and set up the booth, he collected his basket of beef and headed to find Mr. Jenkins to make his weekly payment.

As Caleb wove through the incoming crowd of vendors and customers, Rob walked toward the auction barn. Picking up his pace, Caleb caught up and clapped him on the back. "How goes it, my friend?"

Rob spun to him, and Caleb nearly missed a step. Squelching his shock, he rebalanced the beef basket. Seriously, though, had Rob ever looked so disheveled? How'd he get out of the house without his mom telling him his shirt was on backward *and* inside out? The tag jutting out underneath his Adam's apple had to itch. Just from seeing the thing, Caleb couldn't resist hooking a finger under his own shirt collar and tugging at it.

"It's going." Rob eyed the basket on Caleb's shoulder.

No teasing banter? Where'd the terse response come from? "I'm headed to find Mr. Jenkins and make my weekly payment. Care to join me?"

Rob shrugged. "Sure, whatever."

The drooping shoulders reminded Caleb of when they'd gotten into trouble in junior high. Rob's parents grounded him after the principal told them the boys had been picking on a girl in class. Caleb's parents hadn't grounded him, but the chore list had grown long enough to keep him busy before and after school until dark for two weeks. Something big must be up. "Are you okay, dude?"

"Something got into the garden this week," Rob mumbled. "Broke through the fence and ate the tops off all the beans. I needed to see if we can get any more dried beans from the food pantry to replant."

So that was it. His friend had to ask for help. Stubborn idiot. "Well, you don't need to look all down and out. We've been friends forever. Just ask me. No need to make any official food pantry request. I've got you covered."

But his offer didn't help his friend's disposition. Rob just shrugged and wouldn't make eye contact.

Sure, he was obstinate, but this was taking it to the extreme. "Come on. Let's find Jenkins, then head back to our table."

Caleb couldn't leave his friend all disheveled though, so he yanked on the shirt tag under Rob's chin. Rob's face flamed red as he pulled the shirt off and put it back on correctly.

Mr. Jenkins sat outside the auction barn, watching the various animals troop by, just as he'd told Caleb he would. His cheek bulged with a wad of chaw, and his overalls bore the usual paint speckles.

Last week's delivery basket rested on the ground beside him, so Caleb dropped the full basket and retrieved the empty one.

Mr. Jenkins ogled the basket of beef, spit to the side, and thrust his hand out, and Caleb obliged him with a manly shake. "I have to tell you, I've not eaten beef this tender in longer than I care to remember," he said. "Once this year is over, I may have to find more business to do with you. I don't know that I'll be able to give up the habit I'm going to develop."

His father often received such compliments. Having his own customers, Caleb now realized how important their reputation in the community was. "Good to know our customers are happy with the end product, sir."

Jamming his stained hands into his overalls pockets, Mr. Jenkins bobbed on his heels. "How's the remodel coming along? Have everything you need?"

Caleb explained where they were at in the process but shortened the story when Rob began fidgeting behind him. "All we need is some paint."

With a slow nod and a spit to the side, Mr. Jenkins looked up and to the left. "May have to think on that one for a bit."

As Caleb started back to his family's table, Rob lagged. Caleb paused to allow his friend to catch up, but within a matter of strides, Rob had fallen five paces behind again. This was getting ridiculous.

Caleb stopped and let Rob catch up once more. When his friend reached his side, Caleb punched Rob on the arm—less than gently. "Dude, what's going on with you today? I thought you wanted some beans. You know we've got them. Come on already. The day's wasting away waiting for you."

Rob wouldn't make eye contact. He kicked a stone and watched it fly off. "I don't want charity. I'll trade you for the seeds."

So that was it. The embarrassment of needing charity. Not a problem. "What are you trading, then?"

The stone was under the toe of Rob's left sneaker now. "How about I trade you labor? You need help with that room remodel?"

Yes! Perfect! Caleb could get some help and assist a friend at the same time. "You bet I do. Dad's been helping here and there, but we're both pretty beat after farmwork each day. Can you come this weekend? I'm devoting my whole day Saturday to it."

Rob's head popped up, and his eyes sparked. "Deal—let's get those seeds."

The rest of the way to their table, Rob asked about the remodel and what needed to be done. Wrapped up in their conversation, Caleb didn't notice someone in his path and slammed into her.

Oof.

He recognized the bounce of those curls—Emma. "Sorry about that." He put his hands up, palms forward. "I guess I wasn't paying attention."

She fluffed her hair, then waved a hand. Her lips twisted. "No harm done. I was looking for you, anyway. Fancy running into you—literally."

Rob moved around Caleb, then stepped between him and Emma, his cheesy grin intended for her. "Hey, Emma. Long time, no see."

"Back at ya." She refocused on Caleb. "So, I hear you're doing a remodel."

He didn't recall talking to her about his plan. Maybe Rob had. "It's a project for sure. Can't wait to finish it."

She winked at him, then stepped up to Rob, and hooked her arm with his. "And what are you up to, sport?"

The patches of red that began on Rob's cheeks flushed all the way down his neck as he opened and closed his mouth a few times. "Um, not much."

With poor Rob making a mess of this, Caleb had better save his buddy from himself. He cleared his throat. "So, why were you looking for me?"

Emma seemed to enjoy Rob's discomfort before she refocused on Caleb. "I'm told you're the 'mighty hunter' in the group that killed the pig for the roast. I thought I might make a trade for some wild pig."

"Come on over to the table, and we'll see if there's any left to trade for."

She cocked her hip and held her free arm out to Caleb, making it obvious that she meant for him to take the arm opposite of the one she had clamped to Rob. He switched the basket he carried to the other side.

But they must look stupid, locked together like some strange love triangle. The moment a tight squeeze in their path provided the opportunity, he'd extract his arm from Emma's and walk behind them.

At the table, a crowd had gathered. Some customers were looking to buy, but many were there to talk about the food pantry. They wanted either to donate or to request help.

One disheveled woman in a faded blue dress had a child on her hip, with two in tow. All were dirty and thin, with hollow looks in their eyes. While Mom tended to their needs, he almost swore he saw her slip a gold coin into the woman's pocket.

He hadn't realized how busy they'd be, so he excused himself from Rob and Emma and jumped behind the table to help with customers while Mom and the ladies fielded the food-pantry questions.

By the time the rush was over, they'd either sold or given away every scrap of food on their table. Exhaustion weighed all of them down as they packed up the table along with the empty jars and items taken in trade.

Sitting down in the cart for the long ride home felt wonderful. Oh, man! He twisted his grip on the cart steering wheel. Rob and Emma—he'd completely forgotten about their needs.

Groaning, Caleb lowered his head to the steering wheel.

«»

Later that evening, as he undressed for bed, he checked his pockets before tossing his jeans into the wash. Mom would skin him if he left anything to ruin the laundry. Frowning, he pulled out a folded piece of paper from one pocket. He didn't recall anyone giving him a note or list. He unfolded the note, then froze at the message:

We know what you did to Kacie. If you don't want us to tell everyone, then you'll follow these directions.

This Friday evening, right before dusk, put five pounds of frozen beef on the food pantry's kitchen counter. Leave the key to the back door in the lock. Then go home.

If you tell anyone, we'll expose your secret.

Don't be late.

12

Chapter Twelve

Caleb didn't sleep. The note taunted him. Burying it in his sock drawer wasn't good enough. Still, deep down, he knew he deserved to be found out. Kacie's story needed to be told, including his role.

At the first glint of the sun brightening the treetops, he gave up the pretense and dressed for the day. No sense trying to eat breakfast with the roiling in his stomach, and he couldn't face his family either. Culpability covered his face when he glanced in the bathroom mirror, and he had to look away.

It would be a while until the family was up, so he stepped out onto the back porch and picked up his whittling tools, along with a half-finished wolf whistle. But when he held the wood in his hands, they shook too much to use a knife.

Why did he deserve to continue creating art when his soul was so dark? Instead of a wolf, it should be a darker creature. What was darker than a wolf? Probably a hyena. If he could picture a demon, he'd chisel one of those out of the wood. Perhaps if he could pour it out of his soul into the dead tree, he could purge the darkness from his inner being. He deserved the torture. Why should he enjoy the light when Kacie no longer could?

He dropped the wood back on the side table and stood against the railing while the sun turned the treetops red, then orange, then yellow, eventually showering the trees' true colors with morning light. The slow progression solidified his thoughts.

It had been his mistake. His sin. The family didn't deserve to be weighed down with it. He had to protect them. He'd comply and deliver the meat, leaving the food pantry open for the thieves who'd come. Another treachery he'd have to live with for the rest of his life.

Which was worse—to betray his neighbors' trust or to bring his family's reputation to ruin along with his own? With no good option, he'd protect his family over his neighbors every time he had to choose.

The front door opening pulled him out of his self-loathing. Mom stepped onto the porch, walked up beside him, and threaded her arm around his waist. She was so tiny compared to him. Tenderness welled up in his chest as her dark hair tickled his chin. The role of caregiver had switched. He had to protect her now, whereas she had always taken care of him.

She breathed in deeply, as if drawing the magnificence into her soul. "Beautiful sunrise this morning. I don't blame you for getting up to see it."

If only it were so simple. He could only force one side of his mouth to comply with the commamd to return the grin, and he felt lopsided with the effort. "Not as beautiful as you."

A giggle escaped like she was a schoolgirl again, and she squeezed his ribs. "Your father has taught you well, my son."

She leaned her head against his shoulder as they stared across the back pasture, the tranquility of the cows grazing failing to turn him placid. "What's wrong, Caleb? I can always tell when something isn't right. You've been upset since we came home from the market yesterday. And you *aren't* up with the chickens to stare at the sunrise."

The tension in his body amped up to a new level, and his heart jumped into his throat, threatening to choke him. "Just couldn't sleep, that's all." Just great. His voice had to squeak like those horrid days when it was changing. "Lots to think about."

A tap on his ribs drew his gaze to hers. She seemed to stare into his mind as if she could read his thoughts. He prayed she couldn't. It was too dark, and her soul was too loving.

"There's more to it than simple musings," she said. "I'm married to a man, after all. Women know when the men in their lives are holding back. Moms know even more so."

He forced a smile into his voice and plastered one on his face as well. The motion felt so wrong, but he had to assure her. "I'm good, Mom. The attic remodel, the whittling projects, the farmwork, the food pantry, it's all adding up. Nothing I can't handle, though."

Standing on her toes to reach his cheek, she gave him a peck. "My boy is a man now. I can't protect you from everything, but if I can help with anything, please come to me. Promise you will?"

That he couldn't do. "Love you, Mom."

«»

Friday afternoon, the work party gathered at the food pantry as planned. Several people had agreed to support the effort, and an equal number of people needed the help. A line formed soon after the group arrived at the old house. Mom took control and set a group to work in the back of the house, taking in donations, while another group worked at the front door to allow people in to discuss their needs.

Caleb's job was to direct people to either the front or the back, depending on their requirements. As he dealt with wave after wave, he couldn't clear his mind of what he had to do tonight. The coming betrayal of his family and neighbors felt like an anvil strapped to his waist, weighing him down with every step. Yet how could he not protect them from the truth about who he was, what he was capable of?

His mom, especially, didn't deserve a son like him. She'd raised him to be a good Christian. Someone who honored God and projected God's love like she did. Mom would never understand. How could she?

After the entire day, the lines on both sides of the house dwindled. Exhaustion showed on the team's faces as the last person, an elderly gentleman with faded clothes and worn work boots, walked back up the driveway, heading to his home with a jar of pinto beans and a bag of corn grits.

Dad offered to drive the man home in the golf cart, but he'd waved the offer off. "I may be old, but I'm not dead yet. The walk will do me good."

After shutting and locking the front door, the team gathered on the back porch to enjoy a cooling breeze.

As an owl hooted in the woods, Caleb leaned against the rail, contemplating his dreadful task.

Mrs. Boswell slumped onto a bench. "Now that's what I call a successful day."

Her husband folded his arms across his chest, hip cocked against the porch post. "I can't believe we ended up with more food than we started with, considering how many people came through the front door."

Dad stretched his arms behind his back, then toward the sky, extending his spine up tall. "We must've stacked every jar this county contains—twice."

Mom slumped against Dad after he brought his arms back down, a tired smile easing the cares from her face. "Great job, everyone. I knew it would be a popular place, but I didn't think it would catch on this quickly. I'm so tired—I might go without supper, just for the joy of lying in my bed."

Jan jumped off the stairs on the side of the porch. "Fortunately, Mrs. Dunwoody is cooking tonight, Mom. No worries."

"Ladies, into the golf cart." Dad clapped. "Men, let's take the path through the woods, shall we?"

Caleb followed his father, Mr. Tilbrook, and Mr. Boswell down the path back to their homes. At the edge of the shared property line, the neighbors veered toward their land, waving as they headed home.

The closer they got to their farm, the more nervous Caleb's stomach became. Butterflies weren't just fluttering there—they were rioting and demanding freedom. A plan fixed in his mind, but could he pull it off? Every step toward the house felt like another step closer to his end. How could he come back from doing this to those he loved?

Once they were back at the house, a quick meal of pinto beans and cornbread satisfied their hunger. After asking how Jacob was doing, Jan and Mom recounted opening day. Then Mrs. Dunwoody gushed over hearing how many people had shown up.

Caleb did his best to eat, but the food stuck in his throat. Good thing everyone was too fixated on regaling their stories of the day to notice. With the house enclosed and too warm tonight, almost stifling, it was getting harder to breathe, and his heart rate escalated with each passing moment. He'd need to make his move soon.

To end his torment, he rose from his chair. As he reached for the empty dishes, he said, "I'll clean up tonight, Jan. I know you're tired."

Bewilderment scrunched his sister's face. "Are you feeling okay?"

Shoot. Wrong move. He froze. Then he lifted one eyebrow and held the dishes out toward his sister. "You're going to look a gift horse in the mouth?"

Her confusion ironed out, and she handed him her bowl, the spoon clattering into it. "Nope. I'm outta here." Then she flounced off toward her room.

Concern remained in his parents' eyes, but he ignored them and worked on straightening the kitchen. Mrs. Dunwoody went to check on Jacob while Dad headed out to feed the steers.

Mom hovered, helping Caleb by wiping the table, then the counters. She paused beside him as she rinsed out the cloth in the sink. "When are you going to fess up?"

Whoa. At least, his head faced away from her as he stacked the dishes in the washer. Heat flushed up his neck and over his cheeks. Not daring to look at her, he fussed with the silverware placement. "What are you talking about?"

"A mom knows, son. You should understand that by now."

No way! How could she? "There's nothing to know, Mom. I don't know what you're talking about."

Her hand reached over and rubbed slow circles on his back, as she'd done his entire life to comfort him. The ache in his chest begged for release. Maybe he should come clean.

Mothers always love their sons, no matter what. Don't they?

The gentle soothing ceased, and he wanted it back. "I'm always here whenever you change your mind. I love you, Caleb."

He opened his mouth. Closed it. Swallowed hard. He couldn't change his mind. It would hurt her too much, and she didn't deserve that. "Love you too, Mom."

With a last pat, she left the kitchen, leaving behind a void of compassion. He hardened his resolve, closed the washer, and started it. Then he soft-stepped to the living room where Mom had picked up her embroidery. A piece he hadn't previously seen was in her loom, and she stitched blue threads into the cloth.

It was time.

"Mom, I'm going to check on Max and Luna. I'll be back," he said from outside the room.

"Give them a pat on the head for me," she said without looking up.

He returned to the kitchen and opened the freezer as quietly as he could manage. Stacked packets of beef rested in one compartment, and he removed five of them with slow, stealthy moves, then slid the door closed. As he passed by the key rack, he eased one key to the pantry house off its ring. Since they had spares, maybe no one would notice the missing one.

He'd put his backpack into the golf cart at the beginning of the day, and no one had noticed when he hadn't brought it back in. Opening the pack, he shoved the meat into it and slung it over his shoulders. Although tempted to take the cart, he'd better run the path rather than risk Dad seeing him leaving up the driveway. Maybe a run would even release this pent-up anxiety threatening his sanity.

Max and Luna ran their patrol of the perimeter fences during the day and evenings, and they saw him move along the path toward Mrs. Lancaster's. Excited at the prospect of running with their master, they joined him, tongues hanging out from happy dog grins. They'd bite him if they could understand his mission. He deserved an attack.

At the edge of the clearing by the food pantry, he stopped. The sun hadn't yet set, but that didn't mean people weren't watching. The dogs were busy marking trees and bushes, sniffing for other animal scents. They'd alert if people were in the area. Still, he proceeded to the back door with caution.

The key slid into the lock and twisted. Giving away the hard work of so many was too simple. Inside, the house held a quiet expectation. Even it condemned him with its silence.

He unloaded the backpack onto the counter and eyed the food intended for those who had nothing. His stomach clenched, and bile rose in his throat. It was so unfair. The key snapped against the counter as he laid it beside the meat, still frozen solid. The sound was so final. He wouldn't be able to undo this once it was done.

As he exited the building, he had to close the door with more force than he wanted to since the latch refused to engage with a gentle push. Great, even the house was giving him one last chance to change his mind.

But it was too late. The deed was done. He'd sold his soul to an unknown devil. The punishment was late to arrive, but it was just. Time for him to suffer as Kacie had.

13

Chapter Thirteen

Another sleepless night. The saying—no rest for the wicked—must be true. Staying in bed and pretending to sleep was all he could do. Actual sleep would've been a blessing, not that he deserved one. Dragging himself into the bathroom at sunrise was a task. The dark circles under his eyes would be a dead giveaway to the whole family. How long could he keep the pretense up?

As he trudged from the bathroom back to his bedroom, Mrs. Dunwoody's quiet voice drifted by, talking to Jacob. It was so wrong for the boy to be sick still. How long could the little guy run a fever without permanent damage?

No. Caleb couldn't think that way. Jacob had suffered enough in his brief life. Losing his father, being abandoned by his mother, then being taught to steal by his uncle, like some sort of Oliver Twist knockoff. Jacob deserved to enjoy his new life on the farm, safe again with his mother.

Caleb closed his bedroom door behind him. Overwhelmed, he sank to his knees on the Alabama State Hornets' rug near his bed, planted his palms on the wasp wings, and whispered,

"God, I don't even deserve to pray to you right now. It's not like we've been talking regularly, though Mom would like us to. I won't ask for anything for me. We both know I deserve nothing. But Jacob needs you. I'm asking for him. Please heal him so he can grow up and have his own kid someday."

Mom would advise him to go further with the prayer, but he couldn't. "Amen."

He'd left so much unsaid. It would have to stay that way because it was time to face the music. The waiting game was on. Who would uncover his deception? When would they discover the break-in?

He laughed a tired huff. What break-in? He'd given them the key.

"Caleb," Dad hollered from below. "Breakfast—now."

Caleb grabbed his ASU ball cap off the dresser and crammed it on his head, the hornet on its bill buzzing in his skull. "Okay. Let's do this."

«»

Caleb ran through the list of chores in his head. The herd had to be moved to new pastures today. Every week, they shuffled the two separate herds from one pasture to the next. Eight paddocks divided the farm into sections. Each of them contained enough square footage of grass to keep the small herds content for a week. Then each rotated into a new area.

Because of the cycling process, each field had three weeks to grow back before the herd returned, maintaining the pastures' health. It also prevented the cows from becoming bored, which could cause all kinds of poor behavior. The teenagers, as Dad called them, would get rambunctious and break fences when they grew tired of an area. Variation prevented the need for repairs.

Caleb drove the golf cart out to their farthest north pasture. Such a blue-skied, sunny day normally lightened his mood. If stress didn't weigh on him, he'd drive the farm's perimeter looking for the dogs, just to play a quick game of fetch. Max and Luna loved playtime. Today, though, he went straight to the gate separating the two fields, opened it wide, and yelled, "Here, cow."

A sprawling pin oak stood just inside the fence. Below it, the grass was barren from the combination of the tree's shade, and the trampling the ground took from the cows seeking a cool reprieve. He parked the cart under the tree, got out, and grabbed a bucket from the seat behind him. Some corn mixed with the oats, so when he shook it, a Moroccan rhythm echoed across the property.

"Here, cow. Come on. New pastures." He yelled over and over, rattling the bucket's contents. Soon, the herd moved out of the pines near the field's opposite edge and headed his way. They had trained the cows to come when called. Though the animals didn't often get any of the grain, they'd received the treat often enough to be tempted by the sound.

Once the group was almost to the pen's exit, he got into the cart and circled behind the animals. A quick run around the perimeter proved none were lagging. Excited by the gate opening into the fresh grassy area, the steers broke into a gallop. Younger calves scampered on the heels of the teens, and mother cows with newborns took up the rear. How the herd would separate itself into these groupings, just like humans did, still amazed Caleb.

As the last of the herd filed through the gate, he rode up behind them to close and latch the entryway, then started toward the pasture where the second herd waited. The dinner bell clanged from the house. Someone needed help, and the alarm resonated in his chest, driving his heartbeat faster.

Now what?

He changed trajectories and headed back. As he drew closer, the person on the porch wasn't who he'd have expected to see. Rob stood there, clanging the bell with all he had.

Caleb pulled up and jumped out as Rob rushed to him, words tumbling out of his mouth. "It's the food pantry. Someone broke in and stole everything!"

Everything? Then why ask for the key? Caleb's heart threatened to burst with the heavy pounding. He'd hoped they'd skim some off the top. If they'd done that, they might have gotten away without being discovered. Now everyone would investigate. Would his family notice the missing key? Would they recognize they were short on beef in the freezer?

Rob grabbed Caleb's shoulder. "Dude. Are you listening? Your mom wants everyone to meet up in the dining room. Your dad's already in there."

They started toward the side door, the only unlocked door during the daytime. "Wait." Caleb stopped. "What are you doing here?"

"Remember our garden? You were supposed to get me some bean seeds, but you got all wrapped up in the food pantry work."

Heat seared Caleb's cheeks as he kneaded the back of his neck, recently shaved hair poking at his fingers as his hand moved to the base of his skull. He'd forgotten his friends' needs. "Oh, man. Sorry."

"I figured you'd remember and bring some over, so I waited... and waited." Head ducked, Rob scuffed his feet in the grass, digging a dandelion out with his toe. "We couldn't wait any longer, so Mom and I walked over this morning while you were out working. Mrs. Dunwoody led us over to the pantry, and we found someone had emptied the place out."

Caleb's face burned hotter. The temptation to confess what he'd done knotted his chest. Rob would help him figure out how to get out of this mess or at least be a confidant, helping to shoulder the burden. After all, Rob knew his dark secret.

But Caleb couldn't do it, couldn't admit he'd ruined everything again. Even friendships had a limit and an uncrossable line.

"I can't believe I forgot about you. I'm so sorry." He tried to make eye contact, but Rob wouldn't look up from the ground. "Let's see what we need to do."

«»

They arrived at the food pantry as a group, filing in the unlocked back door and wandering through the empty house as if searching for hidden items. But nothing hid within the four walls. It was all gone, taken by the thieves. Caleb's stomach roiled, and he wanted to punch something—someone.

Then they all gathered in the empty living room, forming a circle with no one directing the action. Mom's shoulders shook as Dad pulled her into his side.

"How could someone do this to us? To our community?" She sobbed between words. "And how did they get in? I don't see anything broken on the doors. Did we leave it unlocked?"

"No way." Dad practically growled the words. "I checked the locks before we left."

Jan's eyes watered as she hugged her arms across her chest, but she jutted out her chin as if she wouldn't let the betrayal defeat her spirit. "It's okay, Mom. We'll collect more. So many people helped before. They will again."

"I'm certain they will." Mr. Tilbrook spoke up. "If we can provide some sort of guarantee, this won't happen again." He looked at each of the men, including Caleb, as if to enlist them in protecting the site.

"Yeah." Mr. Boswell's eyes lit. "We'll keep watch from now on. No way will anyone take us by surprise again. The thieves waited until we were gone. Cowards. Well, we've got the home-court advantage."

Dad gave Mom a squeeze. "Let's put together a schedule. We'll take shifts, two at a time, and we'll teach Max and Luna to include this property in their perimeter checks. They won't get away with this a second time."

Caleb gritted his teeth. He may have caused this, but no way would he allow it again. Still… how had the thieves placed the note in his jeans pocket? He ground his teeth and clenched his fists, his anger fueling a need to know who was behind the blackmail. He'd find out and kick their butts. No one would hurt his family like this again.

«»

The evening's silence broke with the eerie howl of a coyote in the not-so-distant woods. Caleb shivered, thinking of the calves in the fields, but they were all big enough to run to the herd if chased. Most likely, coyotes would focus on smaller prey, though the rabbit population grew smaller by the day. It had been at least a month since he'd seen any on the farm, or even in the gardens, outside of the ones Jacob and Jan were breeding in cages.

The pile of wood shavings grew under his feet. He'd sat on the back porch from the moment dinner ended until now, just after sunset. He whittled by the light emanating from the house rather than turning on the porch lights. Somehow, sitting in the dark seemed appropriate, matching the blackness swirling inside him.

The door swung open, and Mom stepped out, a mug of tea in hand. "Beautiful night, hmm?"

He tipped his head up at the stars he hadn't taken the time to view. Only wisps of clouds moved through the sky, causing stars to disappear and reappear with their movement. A lovely sight he didn't deserve to enjoy.

Whistles wouldn't make themselves, so he refocused. "Yeah. Pretty."

Mom stepped over to the bench he sat in the middle of. "May I?"

Sliding over, he shuffled his foot over the pile of wood shavings to clear a path for her feet.

She sighed as she joined him. "How come you aren't working on your apartment? You're normally eager to spend your evenings up there." Tapping his leg to capture the attention of his eyes, she finished, "What gives?"

Shaking his head, he allowed his gaze to find hers. "How can I, Mom? They took everything. I need to help get the pantry refilled. This isn't the time to be selfish and focused on my own projects."

Her eyebrow twerked toward her dark hair as she drew another sip from her mug. "Really? It's not your fault someone broke in and stole the food. God will provide for us. He always has. You don't have to fix this on your own."

A huff of a laugh escaped before he could shut it down. If she only knew. *God* had provided, and *Caleb* had ruined it. "Perhaps God will provide because I'm going to work for him."

Her hand reached over and rubbed circles on his back. It reminded him of when he was little and Mom's touch was the salve for every wound. She could kiss boo-boos and make them better. At night, she could sing to stop the boogeyman. Her back rubs eased the pain of fights with friends. But her touch couldn't fix this. If he didn't keep her away, she might end up getting burned by his betrayal. She didn't deserve what he offered as a son.

Her hand stilled. Then she slapped him, hard, between the shoulder blades. "Wake up, Caleb."

The blow didn't hurt as much as startled him. She had his full attention now.

"What?"

Mom rose and faced him with her hand landing on her hip. Her flashing eyes meant business. "I don't know what's gotten into you, but it couldn't be any more obvious that the bee in your bonnet has flown up your derriere. I told you before—I know something is wrong." She strode to the door, opened it, and glared at him with a final admonishment. "Someday you need to learn to come clean to your family so we can help you. You can't conquer the world on your own, son. Deal with it."

The door slammed behind her.

His whole body went taut. Only a few times in his life had he seen his mother that angry, and even fewer times had she been angry with him or his sister.

He'd done it up good this time. He stiffened his shoulders and glared at the howling wolf, part of him wanting to howl with it.

But her anger still beat her disappointment if she knew the truth.

14

Chapter Fourteen

Caleb's tight chest loosened when Jacob made it down to breakfast. Pale and weak, the boy wobbled in his seat, eyes alight over being back with the family after weeks in quarantine. The fear of the variant's return had nipped at Caleb, but no one else had fallen ill. They were past it, having dodged a viral bullet.

Caleb ate fast. Once again, market day included hauling a steer to the auction, so everyone from their tight-knit group was helping to load both the truck and the golf cart. As soon as they restocked the food pantry, some would have to stay behind to guard it, but since it was empty, the entire gang could ride along.

Mom had them load the truck bed with extra food from their stock before leaving the house. It wouldn't all fit in the golf cart he'd be driving. "Hungry people will be looking for the food giveaway," she'd said. "Even though we can't provide for all of them, we can make a dent in the need."

Caleb had been in the kitchen earlier in the morning as she brought meat from the chest freezer to the refrigerator's smaller one. "I thought for sure we had more than this," she'd said to him. "But I guess we used it."

The ever-present knot in his stomach clenched tighter. He'd been a weak-kneed fool for allowing the blackmailer to control him. There were other ways to get out of paying off the devil. If another note arrived, he'd change his response.

Now, as they worked to set up the market table, people arrived every few minutes, eager to make a request or drop off donations.

After he placed the final crate back into the cart, Caleb stood behind the table with his whittling projects on the far end. He'd donate whatever he collected to the food pantry efforts. It would take him forever to replace what the thieves stole, but he'd try. His apartment project could stay on hold while he worked on new pieces to sell. The wolf whistles were popular with the kids, so parents and grandparents sought them out for special events like birthdays.

"Well, hello again." Emma emerged from the crowd gathered in front of the tables.

Her smile, seemingly only for him, dried his throat out like a desert. "Hey, Emma." The words croaked out of his mouth. More evidence of his brilliant conversational skills.

She moved around the table to stand beside him. "You going to be busy all day? I wouldn't mind spending some time shopping together."

What a temptation! His every muscle loosened, and he rubbed the bristly short hairs at the back of his neck. It'd be so nice to walk away from his family and friends and forget his worries. Let himself drown in her attention. He eyed the line of people waiting to discuss food pantry issues and then his whittling projects. Sweat beaded his forehead as war broke out between the desire to step away from reality and the need to make up for his deception.

"I *can't.*" He huffed his frustration. "We had a break-in at the food pantry, and I need to get some of this stuff sold to help."

Emma pushed her bottom lip out into a pout. "Really? No one else can help?"

She ran a finger up his arm, tracing a line from his biceps to his right earlobe, which she gave a gentle flick.

Oh, wow. His thoughts jumbled into static, as if his brain was a radio station and his body a truck going into a tunnel. He looked into her eyes—huge mistake. The blue pools further disrupted his thoughts, and his hands felt clammy. So he jammed them into his pockets.

A shove from his left shook him free from her gaze. When he turned to see who had rammed him, Renee was picking up the serving utensils for a wooden salad bowl she'd knocked askew.

"Sorry, Caleb." She dropped the serving spoons back into the bowl. "I tripped over the crate."

Her cheeks flushed as she pushed the errant container back underneath the table where it should have been. Then she smiled without making eye contact. "I wanted to see if you needed any help today."

"Oh, that's so sweet of you." Emma slid her arm around his arm on his opposite side, leaning across him to address Renee. She rubbed her hand up and down Caleb's arm. "We were talking about taking a quick walk around the market. If you could watch his stuff for him, that would be so amazing, wouldn't it, Caleb?"

Those eyes. They were staring right through him. How could eyes as blue as a cool lake cause fire in his throat, drying it completely out?

"Yeah," he said to the eyes, then caught himself. Renee. He should respond to Renee. So he tipped his head her way as the kid smiled beatifically at him. "I mean, yes. That would be awesome if you'd watch this stuff for me."

He breathed in the sweet scent of lilac radiating from Emma, not sure who he was talking to when he added, "We won't be gone long."

Emma's grin widened, and she slid her hand down his arm until it snagged his. Then she led him away from the table, his responsibilities, and every care in the world.

«»

He'd lost track of time, but they must have circled the market a few times, looking at items for sale. It had been the longest he'd ever held a girl's hand as they moved around the market area. It felt wonderful, like he was showing off a prize he'd won.

They were approaching the far edge of the field for another round when Caleb saw Rob and Olivia setting up a table to sell firewood with his parents.

"Let's stop over and say hi." He nudged Emma along, then joined up with his friends. He slapped Rob's shoulder. "Whatcha up to?"

Both Olivia and Rob stared, laser-focused, on their joined hands. Caleb dropped Emma's hand, remembering his conversation with Olivia while they helped Jacob catch fireflies and how Rob and Emma disappeared together that night. How could he have forgotten all that happened then? For all he knew, Rob and Emma had more going on than he realized.

"Afternoon, Caleb," Olivia then nodded to Emma.

Emma returned her nod before winking at Rob. "How are

you today? Get any new mason jars lately?"

Rob glowered. "Not a one. You?"

The vibe between the two felt tense—perhaps a lot more than he thought. What was up with Emma? Did she just hold anyone's hand and flirt? What was the talk about the mason jars all about? Was she his source for the moonshine?

Emma thrust her hip out to the side, sliding both perfectly manicured hands onto her slim waist. She gave Rob a crooked grin. "I saw a few somewhere here. I'll see if I can remember where and get you hooked up again."

Caleb now felt like an outsider, not understanding the undercurrent between the pair. Were they together, or weren't they? Rob acted as if Caleb was trying to poach his girl. But Emma acted as if she were a free agent, not a girl spoken for.

Olivia tossed her hair back. "Whew, sure is hot out today, eh?"

Her long, slim fingers pulled the tresses behind her head, twisted the whole sheet of them up into a bun, and wrapped a scrunchie around the knot to keep it in place. "Don't know if we'll sell much firewood in these temperatures, but if you two know of anyone who's looking, we're going to be here every week from now on. Have to find some way to keep the cupboards from being empty."

Her smile crinkled up a smear of dirt on her cheek. How adorable. Caleb grinned and pointed to his cheek, hoping she'd get the nonverbal hint.

She squinched her eyes.

He was about to reach out to wipe off the smudge when Emma stepped between them.

"You've got enough dirt to pave the highway there, my friend." Emma took her palm to Olivia's face.

By the time Emma finished scrubbing at the smear, a reddened cheek had replaced it. Since Olivia's entire face had gone red, the shade was most likely not from Emma's rough handling. Didn't seem the gesture was as friendly as Emma claimed.

"Thanks." Olivia palmed the reddened area.

Emma's satisfied smirk belied her response. "What are friends for?"

With the atmosphere charged enough to electrocute the four of them, he'd better change the subject.

"They've got the food pantry table going again today, Rob," he said as Emma sauntered to his side and clasped his arm. He peeled her arm back off his, trying to dissuade her from reattaching. "You've been skunked twice now. Do you still need those seeds? Mom brought some."

Now Rob's face caught the beet-colored contagion. "No, we're good. Your mom hooked us up after the break-in."

Whether his friend displayed such embarrassment over the idea of needing help from the food pantry or from Emma's attempt at claiming Caleb's arm, this whole mess was beyond uncomfortable. Why did Emma have to send so many mixed signals? She made it too confusing for his brain to parse. Would he ever understand what women were thinking?

Olivia swatted at her pants as if to dust them off. "I helped get the seeds replanted. I'm looking forward to seeing the garden sprouting. My family never tried to garden. It's an adventure."

She was so perky and upbeat. He couldn't help but smile back at her. "Well, if you are that excited about gardening, why don't you have Rob bring you over to the farm? You can help with the garden work any time. There's plenty to go around."

Her eyes widened, and her smile took over her entire body as she bounced on her toes and scooted closer to Caleb. "I'd love to come over. Can I help feed the cows too?"

"I'm certain we could manage an impromptu feeding, though honestly, they eat grass this time of year."

Emma slid a foot in front of Caleb as if to block Olivia's advance. "I'm sure cow feeding and weed pulling must be exciting, but I'd rather not smell like a barn. Perhaps we should plan another pig roast."

Seeming to like this idea, Rob rubbed his hands together and elbowed Caleb. "Think your dad would take us on another hunt?"

That so wasn't a good idea. The excursion used up too much fuel, and they had plenty of canned pork in the pantry, besides a full freezer. No way would Dad waste fuel to go shoot one pig for entertainment, and a roast had no purpose other than getting friends and family together.

"I don't think that'll happen any time soon. Plus, we're loaded down with harvesting, weeding, and restocking the food pantry—and I've got my whittling and remodel to focus on."

"Oh, let me help. I'd be happy to learn how to harvest." Olivia gave a little clap and spun to Rob, her messy bun slipping sideways at her neck. "I can use what I learn to help your parents with their garden. They don't seem to know that much about how to grow stuff, anyway."

Rob's face flushed once more, and he glared as if she'd just insulted the family. "Fine. Whatever. Do what you want."

He pulled his gloves out of his back pocket, shoved his hands into them, and pointed at the woodpile behind them. "We need to get this wood sold today. It cost Dad a lot to have it delivered here to sell. We can't come home without it all being gone and with cash in our hands."

Olivia nodded. "You're right. I'll start walking around the tables. See who might be interested." Then she tightened her scrunchie to straighten her bun, ducking her head. "It was good seeing you again. I hope I can make it over to the farm soon."

Caleb knew when his friend was in a mood. Best to let him cool down. Plus, Caleb had already spent too much time goofing off. He needed to get back to his table and help. "Later, guys."

Olivia gave him a wave. Rob pretended not to have heard him. Just as well.

"Shall I walk you back?" Emma turned with him toward his destination.

"No, I'd better go solo for the rest of the day." At the disappointment thinning her lips, he plastered a grin on his face. "But I enjoyed our morning together. Maybe next time, okay?"

"Definitely next time." She winked one of those beautiful blues, then sauntered in the opposite direction. He sure would like to figure her out. Or at least understand who she wanted to be with. Befuddled by her mixed signals, he scratched at the ear she'd flicked earlier, then huffed. *Women.*

15

Chapter Fifteen

The attic space was coming along, slowly turning into a completed living area instead of unfinished rafters. Caleb's chest was heavy as he worked on the apartment early in the morning. He should be whittling or working on the farm to help restore the food pantry supplies.

During their breakfast talk, Dad had insisted he take the time for his project. "Son, you need to finish what you've started. Your work to help restore the food pantry is noble, but you've got to take time for yourself so you don't get burned out."

Noble. He knew better than to let that word settle in. If Dad knew why he worked so hard on his whittling, he'd insist Caleb work twice as hard. Because of his stupidity, everyone was working harder to increase the yield and preserve more food.

They hadn't realized how important the food pantry would become in such a short time. The market table crowds kept everyone busy until it got too dark to keep going. Not only was the need tremendous, but also the number of people willing and able to share was astonishing.

"Caleb, you've got company." Jan's head bobbed up and down

at the dumbwaiter entryway.

It drove him nuts when she did that. Jacob had discovered the trick of raising and lowering the lift so he'd be in Caleb's space, then out—up, then down. He'd shown Jan how to do it, and they'd gone into laughing fits at Caleb's annoyed glares, getting a kick out of ticking him off.

He sighed and spread some joint compound over the wallboard joints. "Who?"

Rob's voice came from below. "Who do you think, ya knucklehead? Were you expecting the queen of England?"

His friend's annoyance brought a guffaw to Caleb's lips. "Come on up."

Jan's head disappeared as the lift descended to the second floor. Then, when the elevator rose again, Rob's face appeared. After the dumbwaiter was fully in the room, Rob stepped into the attic apartment. "I see you're making progress. Need a hand?"

Caleb pointed to the bucket of tools by the door. "Sure, grab a spreading knife and get to work. Plenty of work to go around."

After digging around in the bucket, Rob found the tools he needed and joined Caleb. He scooped a glob of the compound out of the five-gallon pail with a large spreader and used a smaller one to apply the compound to a newly papered seam.

They worked silently in the heat of the room, both preoccupied. The small windows were open to let out the fumes from the spackling compound, but no breeze helped with the air exchange.

Rob spoke first. "Brought Olivia with me. She's going out with Jan to the garden."

Caleb's hand stilled. He'd forgotten his promise to show

Rob's cousin around the farm. Just as well that his sister was going to take her. "Jan'll show her the ropes. She loves having people around. Gives her someone to gossip with."

Except for the zone near the ceiling, Rob finished the seam he'd started on, so he grabbed a stepladder and climbed it to reach the upper areas. "Well, all Olivia talked about on the walk over was you. Honestly, she seems a bit obsessed. I don't get why, with your ugly mug."

The laugh that spilled out was automatic. They were back to throwing verbal jibes as they had for years. It felt like normal. The first in a long while. But what about the look Rob had given him when he held hands with Emma? "So, what's up with you and Emma? I didn't think you two were an item, because she grabbed my hand first. But the look you gave us made me think I was wrong. What gives?"

Rob said nothing, as if testing his words in his head before sharing them. Then he climbed back down the ladder. "She's pretty, isn't she?"

What kind of answer was that? "Yes. Beautiful. So, what gives?"

Rob moved to the next seam and began applying more mud. "I don't know if she knows who she wants to be with. Do you? She sure seemed to be into me at the pig roast, but when I saw her holding your hand, she seemed into you. No hard feelings."

No hard feelings? What was going on? Caleb stopped working. "I didn't know you had feelings for her. I just assumed… I mean… I'm sorry, man."

A huffed laugh escaped Rob's lips. "Funny how you can be my best friend and my worst enemy some days. What's that term we used to use? Frenemy?"

A knot tightened up Caleb's stomach. He couldn't just stand

there, waiting for Rob to look him in the eye, so Caleb returned to the wall seams, picking a new one to work on that moved him farther away. "Why would I be your enemy? We've been friends forever."

"Really? Can't you see it?" Rob stopped scraping compound over the paper tape. "Olivia can't stop talking about you, and Emma grabbed your giant paw as soon as she could get her hands on you. She was with me for one evening because I shared my moonshine. But the moment you step foot into the market, Emma's at your side. I can't compete with someone like you."

The smoldering knot in Caleb's gut caught fire, heat rising to his face. "We're not competing. I said I was sorry. I'm not trying to steal your girl. I didn't know."

Rob tossed his spackling blades onto the floor. "Yeah? Well, it doesn't much matter now, does it? She's obsessed with you."

Frustration at his friend's stubbornness stoked the flames in Caleb's belly. "Don't be an idiot. I won't spend any more time with Emma. Not now that I know. Let it go."

Saliva flew out of Rob's mouth, peppering the drywall with his next words. "Easy for you to say, *friend*." He wiped his mouth and stormed over to the dumbwaiter. "I've gotta go. My parents need help in our garden if we're going to feed ourselves this winter. Walk Olivia home when she's done here. She'd rather be with you, anyway."

Caleb tried to reason once more. "Oh, come on, dude. Cut it out."

But Rob had already begun his descent.

"Really?" Caleb shouted toward the disappearing elevator. "Ugh!" He threw his compound blade at the drywall, and a splatter of spackling mud ricocheted back to pelt him with speckles in the face and chest.

Great. Now he had a mess to clean up. If he didn't get the joint compound off the wall soon, he'd be sanding it off. And if he didn't get Rob to accept his apology, he'd be fighting to get his best friend back.

All this over a woman. Why hadn't he kept a cool head? Emma had a way of getting into his brain, putting a stop to rational thought. There had to be a way to short-circuit her advances. Though, if she was being such a flirt with other guys, why would Rob want her, anyway?

Right. He knew why Rob wanted her. She was gorgeous and sophisticated. Candy for the eyes and ears.

Enough. He had work to do. He sighed, scowling at the spattered wall, already drying in spots. When he took Olivia back, he'd get his friend to listen.

«»

Lunch was normally around one o'clock. This time of day grew too hot to garden. They tried to get all outside work done early in the morning, another reason Caleb felt so guilty spending his morning working on the apartment.

Dad had already hollered up that it was lunchtime, and Caleb knew better than to keep his father waiting for food. Mom would insist all were present for a blessing before anyone got to eat.

After he'd sealed the lid on the compound bucket, Caleb used the dumbwaiter to descend to the second floor and washed his hands in the bathroom. He walked into the dining room as Mom put the steaming pot of pinto beans on the table next to the glass pan of cornbread.

Jan and Olivia sat across the table from Jacob and Mrs. Dunwoody, and Dad reigned supreme at the head of the table, as usual. Caleb took the chair next to Mom.

She held out her hand for him to clasp. Once they all joined hands around the table, she prayed. "Father, we thank you for a successful morning of work. Having Jacob back at our table is an added blessing, and we ask that you continue to heal him so he can join in the work again. Please nourish us with this food so we can work for you some more this afternoon. In Jesus's name, we pray, amen."

They all chorused, "Amen."

Jacob must feel better since he grabbed a piece of cornbread and stuffed half of it into his mouth, then crumbled the remaining half into his bowl. Mrs. Dunwoody poured a scoop of the pinto beans on top of it and Jacob mixed the two together before he began shoveling the food into his mouth.

Yup. The kid was feeling better, for sure.

Jan handed her bowl out for Caleb to serve her. After her bowl was full, she addressed the group. "Olivia is a mad fiend in the garden. I've never seen anyone weed a row of beans so fast in my life."

The smile curving up Olivia's cheeks brought a heat to his belly as she pulled her cap down lower to hide her eyes. Her soft response was almost a whisper. "Just doing my part."

Dad's bowl contained two crumbled hunks of cornbread Caleb smothered in pinto beans and sauce. The bread soaked up some of the liquid from the beans. After he scooped a spoonful into his mouth, Dad chewed, swallowed, and pointed his spoon at Caleb. "Make some good progress on the apartment today?"

"Yes, sir." He served his share of beans and mixed in his cornbread. "The joint compound is drying. Should be ready to sand the next chance I get to work on it. I was going to reset the gate into the orchard this afternoon. A steer knocked it off the hinge, but I didn't have a wrench with me yesterday when I found it."

"You can take care of that after you drive Olivia home. It's a bit too hot for her to walk today, and I don't need the golf cart this afternoon."

"Yes, sir. I'm on it."

Olivia blushed. "Thank you."

Man, those pink cheeks were so adorable. It was as if she were flowering into a carnation with the attention.

After the meal, he trailed Jan and Olivia out to the golf cart, Jan's enthusiasm evident in her skip as she walked backward facing her new friend. "Come back any time. I know it's a hike to get here, but if you walk through the edge of the woods, it isn't as hot."

He thrust his hands into his pockets and scuffled his feet, kicking up red dust as Olivia and Jan wrapped each other in a hug as if they'd become best friends during their morning work and wouldn't see each other again for years. Then Olivia climbed onto the passenger seat, and he took over at the wheel. "Ready?"

That sheet of silky hair she'd let loose shone as she nodded. "Ready." Then she waved to Jan, who backed away from the cart. "I'll be back to help some more. Just have to make sure they don't need me at home tomorrow."

As they backed out of the carport, Jan gave her new confidant a quick wave before heading into the house to conquer the lunch dishes.

"Thanks for giving me a ride home, Caleb." Olivia palmed flyaway wisps of hair away from her cheeks, then held them down with one hand. "I could have walked, really. I know you'd rather be working on your apartment."

"It's all good." With one hand on the wheel, he relaxed back into his seat. "I need to talk to Rob again, anyway."

She then peppered him with questions about the remodel and what the finished apartment would look like. It was a pleasant conversation, and her enthusiasm revived him.

As they pulled into the Jacksons' driveway, Rob's parents were working in the garden, but there was no sign of his friend. They got out and joined Mr. and Mrs. Jackson, who were running VCR tape around the perimeter of their food plot.

"What's up?" Caleb toed a clod of weeds one of them must have tossed from the garden earlier.

Mr. Jackson wiped his soggy brow with his shirt sleeve. "We heard these old VCR tapes are good to keep the deer out. Hopefully, the combination of the noise in the wind and the literal barrier will protect our second planting. We can't afford to lose the entire crop again."

"I know what you mean. Hope it works." Caleb gestured toward the house. "Rob home?"

Mrs. Jackson stooped to rearrange the tape around a thin pole that rose from the ground. "You know the way. He headed toward his room the last I saw him."

Yup, he knew the way. He'd spent many hours over the years at his friend's house. The Jacksons were like his second parents. When he arrived at Rob's room, the door was closed, so he knocked. "Dude, you dressed?"

After some shuffling on the other side, the door opened. Rob's eyes were unfocused under his shaggy bangs. So he'd found more moonshine. Why didn't Mr. and Mrs. Jackson address the issue?

Caleb let out a long breath. "Can we talk?"

In an unexpected rush, Rob grabbed him into a bear hug. "Of course. Sorry about earlier. I was out of control."

Even with the sudden turnaround throwing Caleb's mind into a confusing muddle, he wasn't about to look this gift horse in the mouth. He pounded on his friend's back, jostling the scowling bulldog stamped on his sweat-stained Nike shirt. "It's all good, man. I'm sorry too."

It was good to be back with his friend. He wouldn't let Emma come between them again. He was done with trying to figure her out. Rob could have her.

16

Chapter Sixteen

On his turn to serve guard duty at the food pantry, Caleb was grateful for his father's company. Being on alert and wielding the rifle with his handgun belted to his waist brought back uncomfortable memories of the marauders' attack. It seemed the world would never return to normal, but having to be an armed protector of food stores for the poor was just plain over the top.

They'd already been on guard half the night, and technically, it was already morning—extremely early in the morning. It had been quiet, and Dad rejoined him on the back porch. Most of the night, they'd each guarded one end of the house to ensure no one could sneak through the building's opposite doors.

He ought to be grateful there was food in the building again. When he'd removed his pants the evening after market day, he'd been afraid to check the pockets. Even though he'd been alert for any activity nearby or anyone bumping into him, his relief at finding the pockets empty nearly buckled his knees.

"Earth to Caleb," Dad said. "Did you hear me?"

Shoot. He must have spaced out. "Sorry, Dad. What?"

Dad not so gently smacked the back of his head. "Pay attention. You're on guard duty, not at a bird watching symposium."

Good thing it was dark out, so his embarrassment wouldn't be as evident. His father was right. He had to get out of his head. "Yes, sir."

"I said I'm going to check out the front of the house again. It's doubtful the thieves will come back now that we're on alert, but you need to listen for any sounds or movement."

Dad strode away with quick but quiet footfalls. Stiff from standing in the same position for too long, Caleb stretched his neck and then his back. Small pops emanated from his joints, and he rotated each shoulder, continuing the movements to limber his muscles and refresh his tired brain.

A tap sounded from the nearby wood line. Was it a tap? Or a pop? Perhaps a squirrel dropping a nut from one of the oaks? He walked to the side of the house where Dad had gone. No sign of anyone there. Next, he moved to the other side to peer down the length of the building. No one there either.

Another tap in the woods, then the snapping of branches as something moved through the forest. That was no squirrel. He lifted the rifle to chest level, aiming toward the retreating steps. Sure, the feet were running away from him. But why had they retreated, and what was the tapping about?

The situation tempted him to call his father over to help him inspect the woods, but for all he knew, the person or persons involved were waiting for them to go into the woods so they could go through the front of the building. No way would he let them pull the guards from the food pantry. He'd rather risk a short walk through the front line of the trees.

The sounds were gone now, so whoever had been in the area

moments ago wasn't there anymore. Clouds intermittently hid the partial moon, as they did now, making it hard to see. But it would get light soon, and the trespassers wouldn't be brave enough to show themselves once the sun rose.

He returned to his post in the back, alert to every sound emanating from the forest.

Once the sun came up, Mr. Boswell and Mr. Tilbrook relieved them of their posts.

"Any problems last night?" Mr. Boswell asked as he stifled a yawn.

"None," Dad responded. "It's all yours now."

His father started on the path toward their property, but Caleb had a hunch the tapping last night meant something. "I'll catch up in a minute, Dad. I'm going to check out some noise I heard a few hours ago."

Dad's eyebrows shot up. "Why didn't you say something? We'll look together."

Caleb shook his head. "I'm sure it was a squirrel or a deer playing with my imagination. I just need to satisfy my curiosity at this point."

Though his father's eyebrows resumed a calmer position, he refused to continue toward their home. "Still, I'll go with you."

Shrugging, Caleb moved toward the trees. "Suit yourself."

Once they entered the woods, he pointed toward where he'd heard the noise, and Dad made a motion with his hands that he'd circle around to cover more area. This sent them in opposite directions. Caleb tried to walk softly, though he wasn't certain why. He hadn't heard a thing since the retreating footfalls hours ago.

He must have walked five hundred yards through the woods, seeing nothing out of place. Dad met up with him.

"Anything?" Dad said.

"Nothing."

Disconcerted, Caleb kneaded the back of his neck, cringing when he brushed the bristly hair the wrong way and an involuntary shiver ran down his spine. Had someone snuck up to the house and retreated after realizing it was being guarded? What was the tapping sound then?

Just one more quick look… "I'm going to take one last pass through. Then I'll meet you back at the property line."

"I guess I'll circle back around too, then."

They separated once more and took different trajectories back to their land. He'd just relaxed at not finding anything when a fluttering motion caught his attention. Someone had attached a piece of old notebook paper to a tree. He'd missed it on the opposite side of the tree from what he'd seen on his way in.

Stopping in front of the note, he swiveled his head around in as many directions as he could, twice, searching for any sign of another human in the vicinity. Nothing. Only the lone paper on the tree.

His heart raced. Someone had used a staple gun to attach the note, the obvious source of the popping sound in the dark. But the writing on the front of the folded sheet riled him up. Five big block letters—C–A–L–E–B.

No. It couldn't be. They'd found a way to get a note to him again.

He didn't want to touch it. Somehow putting his hand on it meant it was real. A continuation of the nightmare he'd been living.

"Caleb." His dad hollered from far ahead. "You coming?"

Caleb ripped the note off the tree and crammed it into his

pocket. The pounding of his heart made him woozy, and he reached out for a branch to steady himself. "Coming."

It wasn't fair. Why him?

«»

Back in his room, supposedly to catch a nap, Caleb slid his hand into the offending pocket of his jeans. The note was still there, taunting him. He wanted to tear it into tiny pieces and flush it down the toilet, but feared the repercussions too much not to look. He slid it out, his heart beating in his throat.

Light-headed, he dropped on the edge of the bed, the blanket's heroic black and gold colors mocking his cowardice. His thumb rubbed over his name.

Man up and read it.

He unfolded the note as if a scorpion waited inside, ready to strike the moment he freed its tail. The handwriting was neat.

We haven't forgotten Kacie. Neither has her family. You haven't paid in full yet for your sins. Make sure you're on guard duty tomorrow night. Alone. Then move to the front of the house with the back door open. Leave another five pounds of frozen beef on the kitchen counter.

Tell anyone, and we'll expose your secret to the world.

Such a pity. Such a sweet girl.

So that was it. More blackmail payments were due if he didn't want his parents to know. He let his body fall backward onto the black and gold bedding, threw his arm over his eyes, and crumpled the note in his fist. This wouldn't end unless he ended it. But how? How could he put a stop to it?

One option was to come clean. The truth would devastate Mom. Dad would turn his face away to avoid making eye contact. Jan would cry. He could see her tears already.

How could that be an option?

It wasn't. But what alternative did he have?

A tap on his door jarred him. He jolted upright. "Yes?"

"Can I come in?"

What could Mom want right now? He stuffed the note into his pocket. "Yes, ma'am."

The door swung inward, Mom following its trajectory. She carried a bowl. "I brought up a quick snack for before you go to sleep. You forgot to grab something for breakfast on your way up."

Steam rose from the grits. Just the thought of choking them down turned his stomach. "Thanks, Mom, but I'm good."

She set the bowl on the bedside table, the bowl seeming to crush the hornet on the pennant beneath it. Then the mattress dipped as she sat beside him. Her arm encircled his waist. "What's wrong?"

He eyed her sideways, trying to look as no-nonsense as that hornet. "Why does something have to be wrong? I just stood guard duty all night. I'm exhausted."

Her mouth twisted. "Fair enough. But you're on notice that I expect you'll be eating a full lunch this afternoon. Or else."

"Message received, Mom." He let himself flop back onto the mattress, shutting his eyes on his way down. "Can I go to sleep now?"

She smacked his leg. "I'll put the grits in the fridge for later."

He felt her rise from the bed and heard her pick up the bowl and leave the room. The door clicked as it closed.

Decision time. What was he going to do?

What could he do but sleep on it? Exhaustion kept him from getting any deeper into the thought process.

«»

A bang on the door shocked him awake. "Caleb. Wake up

and let me in. Why did you lock your door?"

It was Mom again. How did his door get locked? He hadn't locked it since he was back in school.

He shot up out of the bed and couldn't find his pants. Where had his pants gone?

More loud banging. "Caleb. Now."

Why was she so angry? He stumbled to the door and fumbled to get it open. It stuck. He yanked and twisted the knob, struggling to free the mechanism, but couldn't make progress. What was going on?

Her voice sounded frantic. "I'm going to find your father if you aren't out here by the count of three, young man."

Ugh, uh-oh. The "young man" was out now. That never ended well. "I'm coming. The door is stuck."

He needed to find pants. The last thing he wanted was to be standing in his underwear when the door freed up.

He moved to his dresser and pulled on the drawer that held his jeans. Jammed.

Next, he tried the shirt drawer. That one wouldn't move either. What was going on? Great, he didn't have a shirt on either. He was standing barefoot in his tighty whities as Mom hollered through the door. "That does it. I'm getting your father."

He moved to the closet to grab a pair of khakis instead of fighting with the drawer any longer. But the accordion door wouldn't budge.

Now what? Was someone playing a trick on him? Had Rob set him up to get even? Jan would love to have fun with him, but this seemed a bit much. Stuck in his room, no clothes, and no way out.

She was probably just outside the door, listening to him

struggle. "Ha. Hilarious, Jan. Unlock the door and toss some pants in here."

But instead of the giggling he expected, someone started crying outside the door. "Jan? Is that you?"

He stepped up closer and put his ear against the door. Yes. It was crying. A girl. "Jan?"

"It's me, Caleb." The voice chilled his blood. "It's Kacie."

His eyelids flew open as he shouted, "No!"

He was lying in the middle of his bed, blue jeans still on, his T-shirt soaked with sweat, his heart pounding. It had been a dream. No—a nightmare.

Rolling over, he pulled the striped black and gold blanket over his head, burrowing in but unable to hide from reality. He'd made his mind up. He couldn't let his mistakes haunt his family like they did him. The blackmailer wouldn't get free access to the food pantry again. He'd figure out who was behind this and put an end to it.

17

Chapter Seventeen

Caleb wandered down to the kitchen for lunch, hair fresh-cut with the trimmer and still wet from the shower. He mentally wrestled with himself about what to do about the note. Part of him wanted to take the extra guard duty and make the payment. It would be kicking the can down the road farther—cowardly, but effective.

On the other hand, he was fed up with the situation weighing on him day in, day out. He couldn't take much more of it.

When he passed through thc living room, Mom was on the couch, stitching away at her embroidery project. The color tone of the threads was much darker than usual. She normally crafted in reds, pinks, and yellows, but this project had navy blue, purple, and hunter green—like a healing bruise. Her embroidered Bible verses were usually gifts since they took her a long time to prepare. She obviously intended this one for a male with its dark hues.

She spoke as he passed by. "Morning, again. You ready for some food now?"

He moved over to kiss her on the cheek as he'd done when

he was small. "Yes, ma'am."

Setting the embroidery aside, she rose and headed toward the kitchen. "Rob and Olivia showed up this morning. They didn't know you had guard duty last night, so they went out to help Jan in the garden again. Renee and Lizzy are out there too."

If the entire gaggle of girls was in the garden, most likely it was more chatter and less weed pulling than normal, so he wasn't regretting having slept in. But garden work was critical to keeping the family fed, as well as supplementing the food pantry, so he'd get his butt out there as soon as he got some lunch.

A thumping on the stairs drew their attention, but Jacob's voice rang out. "It's okay. I just dropped my boots."

Mom shook her head. "Why would Jacob have his boots upstairs? He knows they belong on the rack by the door."

Caleb barked out a laugh. It reminded him of himself at Jacob's age, always doing stuff that riled Mom up. If only his problems were still the small kind… like bringing boots into the wrong part of the house or dropping things down the stairs.

The redhead popped into the room, his grin almost reaching the back of his head. "Mom said I can go out to the garden with you. I've got my boots and everything."

Parking himself on a stool at the kitchen island, Caleb dug a spoon into the bowl of grits his mom had pulled out of the microwave. "Oh really? And why didn't you just go with Jan and the girls?"

Mrs. Dunwoody came in from the laundry room. "That would be because someone didn't want to eat his breakfast this morning."

Alarms sounded in his brain. Jacob not eating his breakfast? Was he getting sick again?

Jacob moaned. "Oh, Mom. You know eggs taste funny. I wanted cornbread."

Caleb chuckled, then relaxed into a full guffaw. "Protein is important, buddy. You can't just eat carbs all day." He spun his chair and grabbed the boy by the arms, lifting him into the air. "You need muscle power."

Laughter spilled out of Jacob. "Put me down. I'll eat eggs tomorrow."

Caleb plopped the boy back down on his feet and tousled his hair. Maybe he should offer to run the trimmer over it since Jacob still hadn't let Mrs. Dunwoody take scissors to it. But the kid would look weird with a buzz cut. "No arguing with your mom."

Mrs. Dunwoody's smile encompassed them both. "He can go out with you if you're headed to the garden."

Returning to his bowl, Caleb retrieved the spoon. "Yes, ma'am. I'm headed out as soon as I finish this."

Jacob jumped up and down like a Mexican jumping bean. "Come on… Let's go."

«»

With the golf cart already out in the garden, Caleb and Jacob walked through the pastures toward where everyone was working. As the sun neared its zenith, the heat was intensifying. He kept a close eye on his mini-man companion for signs the temperature was too much for the boy. So far, Jacob's constant chatter never flagged, and he showed no signs of heat stress.

When they reached the garden, the workers didn't notice them until Jacob hollered out, "Hi, guys!"

Everyone took his arrival as a sign to take a break from

the hot, dirty weed pulling. They gathered around Jacob, patting him on the head and jostling him about as they would a younger brother.

"Good to see you outside again." Jan winked. "Now get to work."

Jacob spun around and jumped. "Just show me where to start. I'm ready."

They all laughed as he grabbed Lizzy by the hand and caught Jan with the other. He dragged them back into the garden to find a row needing weeding.

Rob clapped Caleb on the shoulder. "Long night?"

Man, was it ever. Caleb nodded. "The longest."

Renee whispered something to Olivia, and then both eyed him.

Oh boy. Having the girls whispering was never a good sign. "Morning, ladies." He gave a wave, then cuffed Rob's arm. "Ready to get back at it?"

A frown passed on Rob's face, like he was upset about something, but then let the thought pass. "I'd hoped we'd be working on your apartment today, rather than sweating out here in the dirt."

After a brief look out at the garden and the work remaining, Caleb could justify returning to the house. The girls had the weeds well under control, and the beans would be ready to pick soon—but not yet. The ladies didn't need them today. "We can arrange that. Just let me talk to Jan about watching Jacob."

They walked over to where Jan and Lizzy were helping Jacob with his chosen row. The kid already had dirt in his hair. A mini weed-throwing tournament must have occurred in the recent past. "Jan, we're heading back to the house to work in the apartment. We'll leave the cart, so please make sure Jacob doesn't stay out too long, okay?"

She didn't look up from her task. "Got it."

«»

Once ensconced in the apartment-in-the-making, Caleb tied a rag around his mouth and nose to act as a mask. He pointed to a pile of rags and motioned for his friend to do the same. While Rob picked one from the pile, he didn't tie it to his face. Instead, he slid a flask out of his hip pocket, took a swig from it, then offered it to Caleb.

"No thanks." He set to work sanding down the seams. "If you don't put that mask on, you're going to get a lungful of dust. Put the booze away and mask up."

Rob just shrugged, took another pull, and began twirling the makeshift mask. "What's the point of working at this apartment, anyway? Wouldn't you rather own your own place?"

Heat flared in his brain. Caleb glared daggers at his friend, then resumed sanding. "Yeah, I'd love my own place. Like that's going to happen. So, in the meantime, I'm working on this. What's your grand plan—drown the problems of the day in moonshine?"

The twirling stopped, and the flask returned to Rob's lips once, twice, then a third time for a long pull. He gave the container a quick shake, then upended it, empty. After he stuffed the container into his rear pocket, he crammed his hands into his front pockets and dragged a toe along the floor, clearing a line in the compound dust. "At least I know how to have fun. More than you do. You didn't even notice Olivia and Renee giving you the smitten-kitten look. Emma would rather be with you than me, and you couldn't care less."

The last words came out a bit slurred, and *less* drug out with multiple *S*s on the end, like a snake's hiss.

That was the corker. He'd had enough of his friend's idiocy. Caleb threw the sanding block at Rob's shoulder, hitting him squarely and sending a puff of joint compound dust into the air, coating Rob's shoulder-length hair in a white powder. Caleb advanced, ripping off his makeshift mask and poking his finger into Rob's chest.

"I've had it with your attitude. Ever since you got back to Shiloh, you've been nothing but a pain in my behind."

All the pressure built up from the blackmailer's threats, his friend's drinking, and Jacob's illness was coming out now. His finger jabbed at Rob every few words. "Who do you think you are, anyway? You're supposed to be my friend, supporting me. Instead, you try to get me hooked on that poison you love so much. No wonder Emma wanted to be with me instead of you."

Having a target for his anger felt good, but his friend's eyes hardened. Rob swung at Caleb's finger, slapping it from his chest. "You think Emma wants to be with you? Ha! You think everybody wants to be with you, huh? All the girls should follow you like some sort of pied piper."

Rob turned the attack on Caleb, gait unsteady, until they stood nose-to-nose. Rob's face mottled red underneath the white dust. "I've got news for you, buddy. You may have everyone else fooled, but I *know* who you are. You're no saint. Olivia thinks she's not pretty enough for you. Did you know that?"

Caleb froze in place. Olivia? What did she have to do with any of this?

Rob raised his chin, apparently empowered by Caleb's lack

of response. "That's right. She told me she thought Emma was prettier and had a better chance with you than she did. So, you can have any girl you want, can't you? Renee trips over her tongue just trying to say hello, but you don't even notice, do you?"

Renee? Just what was his friend saying? Rob didn't know what he was talking about. He was such a drunken fool. Caleb twisted the cloth mask in his hands. "Well, you don't deserve any girl, or should I say no girl deserves to be stuck with you. Look at you—you're a mess."

He pushed back against Rob's advances, causing his friend to step backward and trip over a toolbox. Rob fell hard, sending tools skittering across the floor.

Rob's eyes went wide, but he scrambled up off the floor. His eyes narrowed into a glare as he dusted off his clothes, white puffs of compound rising off his pants. "I've had enough of you to last me a good while. Maybe even forever. Be a good pal to your sorry friend and walk Olivia home again this afternoon. But don't break her heart on the way. She doesn't know you like I do."

Caleb clamped his mouth shut, having nothing to say to the idiot making his way down in the dumbwaiter. If Rob could make it back home without falling into the ditch, he'd be one lucky drunk. Come to think of it, Caleb hoped he landed in a ditch. It'd serve the jerk right.

No sense wasting any more time with his so-called friend. Caleb wrapped the rag around his mouth once more and began sanding down the joint compound seams. The frustration overwhelmed him and came out in his arm motions, furiously working down the length of the wall. So, Rob was jealous. That was obvious. Rob must've brought Renee into the conversation to up the ante. Caleb hadn't realized how childish his friend could be.

Well, if Rob wanted it that way, then Caleb could play the same game. The next time Emma showed interest, he was all in. Before his friend had acted like a fool, he was more than willing to step aside and leave the pursuit of the gorgeous blonde to Rob.

Not now. Let the games begin.

«»

Caleb hadn't kept track of the time, but his arms felt like rubber from the workout they'd gotten sanding. White dust covered the room, and it would all need a good cleaning before he could apply the primer. Too bad he still didn't have any paint to finish it. Maybe someday.

The dumbwaiter creaked its way up, announcing a visitor. He'd need some sort of doorbell or communication system once he lived in the apartment. The last thing he wanted was to be running around in his PJs and having someone arrive unannounced. That would have to wait for another day, though. Now, he just looked in that direction to see whose head appeared.

Jan started coughing before the dumbwaiter made it all the way into the room. He hadn't thought about it, but the swirling white cloud around the dumbwaiter meant a lot of debris must be hitting the second floor through the opening. He'd better get it cleaned up before Mom saw it.

Jan had pulled her shirt sleeve over her nose and mouth by the time she was fully in the apartment. Moving her arm away from her face, she said, "Olivia is ready to go home. Where's Rob?"

Olivia. He'd forgotten about her. "I'm coming. Rob took off

early, so I'll walk her home."

He walked over to join Jan in the dumbwaiter and lowered them back to the second floor.

Jan stepped out of the lift. "Everyone's back now, so you can take the golf cart. It should still have plenty of charge left."

The square area around the dumbwaiter opening needed to be cleaned up. "Thanks. If Mom sees this mess before I return, tell her I'll clean it up when I get home."

The drive to Olivia's home was a quiet one. She talked some about her day in the garden and how much she enjoyed working with the other girls. But his mind was on his conversation with Rob, and she'd gone silent. By the time he realized she wasn't talking anymore, he guessed he'd also have to make up for being a poor host at some point. The list of things to make up for was getting way too long for anyone to accomplish.

As he stopped in front of their house, Olivia disembarked. "Thanks for the ride, Caleb. I appreciate it."

"No problem."

"Did you want to come in to see Rob or my aunt and uncle?"

As she latched her hands behind her back and blinked puppy-dog eyes up at him, her sheet of silky hair falling to one side, she looked so hopeful. It was almost too painful. She was too nice to be around someone like him. She needed a nice, clean-cut guy with no history. "No. I need to get back and clean up. Thanks, though."

Those glowing eyes faded, and her lips drooped. "Oh. Okay. I understand. Have a good night."

"Yeah." He put the cart into reverse. "You too."

18

Chapter Eighteen

Somehow, Caleb kept from airing his thoughts that evening when Mr. Jackson and Rob stopped by the farm. They were on their way to the food pantry to relieve the day watch. Rob's head must ache from his afternoon indulgence.

Rather than talk to his former friend, Caleb moved to the back porch to whittle. Dad answered the door when Mr. Jackson knocked, and though Dad invited him in, the pair went out on the front porch instead.

Caleb twisted the knife along the wooden grooves, grinding his teeth against the desire to go out with his father and confront Rob in front of Mr. Jackson about the out-of-control drinking. But he was too angry to be civil. Mom would be furious if he disrespected company. So he sat on the back porch and whittled away.

While the shavings fell to the deck floor, he contemplated what his actions—or lack thereof—meant tonight. He hadn't offered to take over the night watch, as per the blackmailer's instructions. So what would that cause tomorrow morning?

What would happen when the blackmailers showed up and realized he hadn't complied? Would Rob and his dad have problems tonight? That thought settled uneasily in his brain. Was he putting them in danger by not saying anything? What option did he have besides continued payments to the rogues? There were no simple answers and no good way out of the mess he was in.

For all he knew, he might wake up tomorrow and discover the entire world knew his secret. If the truth came out, he'd have to leave his family and live on his own. No way could he look his mother in the eye once she knew.

And what about what Rob had said? *Was* Olivia interested in him? He wasn't the right guy for her. She was too sweet and quiet, delicate, like fine china to his cast-iron skillet. He'd break her too easily.

Renee was practically his kid sister. She and Jan had been best friends for as long as he could remember. Rob had to be wrong about her feelings for him.

Emma seemed more sophisticated in the ways of the world. She wouldn't be a soft touch to anyone. Perhaps she'd be the better target for his affections. Time would tell.

By the time he crawled into bed, his weary brain thrummed. He was stuck like a fly in a tar pit. The ooze from the mistakes he'd made was going to pull him under and drown him for sure.

The fear of what his dreams would bring kept him awake until his body gave out and he drifted off.

When the sun's rays began seeping into his bedroom window, he peeled open his sticky eyes enough to acknowledge the new day, then unfisted his clenched grip from the striped blanket. He didn't hear any commotion to indicate an alarm had gone out about the food pantry being attacked and robbed. That had to be a good sign. Perhaps the blackmailers had given up after they saw he wasn't on guard duty. Could it be that easy?

He couldn't believe market day was here again. By the time he slogged through the routine of dragging his tired body out of bed, putting on clean clothes, and trundling down the stairs, Dad was practically salivating.

"Nice of you to join us for breakfast, son. I thought I'd have to come up and dress you myself."

Jan, Jacob, and Mrs. Dunwoody sat at the table. Scrambled eggs and cornbread muffins steamed hot in front of them.

Mom came in, placed a pot of grits on the table, and took her seat at the opposite end from his father. "Oh, hush, Steve. Caleb's not that late, and the grits just finished, anyway. Now let's ask a blessing."

They joined hands around the table, and Mom prayed. "Father, we thank you for another day and for each person in our circle. Thank you that Jacob is well again and that we've been able to get the food pantry started once more."

Caleb flinched, his hands tensing against Mom's and Jan's.

"Please guide us today and help us make wise choices. Bring those who need our help and those who can assist to our table today. We thank you for the food you so generously give to us that we are about to enjoy. Help it nourish and strengthen us for our day of work. Amen."

The last amen hadn't escaped their lips before Jacob's hand shot out and grabbed a muffin and he chomped into it.

Mrs. Dunwoody eye-rolled at her son's fixation on the muffins. She scooped a portion of the eggs onto his plate. "No more cornbread until you've eaten at least two bites of egg, young man."

Jacob scowled and hunched down, shoulders drooping.

It was all Caleb could do not to laugh at the boy's silent protest.

As Jan served herself a bowl of grits, he caught her holding back a smile. "Dad." She shifted sideways in her chair, perhaps to avoid the eye contact with him that would surely unleash both their laughter. "Jacob and I want to look for a lamb today at the market. Remember, you'd said we could have a few sheep if we took care of them ourselves?"

Dad huffed out a breath. "I remember. But you need to do all the work yourselves, including checking their fencing every day. I've got enough on my hands." He jabbed a pointer finger against the table. "These won't be pets. This is a farm. We grow food on a farm, not playmates."

Jacob sat up straight as an arrow. "Yes, sir." He shoveled egg into his mouth with one hand and snagged another piece of cornbread with the other.

Jan was going to be a great mom someday. She knew how to maneuver the boy into doing whatever needed to be done. Smart girl, that one.

Dad raised a heavy brow Caleb's way. "We're selling some heifers at auction today."

Caleb's fork with a bite of grits stilled midway to his mouth. "Heifers?" Since they were growing a second herd with a second bull, they sold the steers and kept the heifers sired by one bull to mate with the second in future years. "Why's that?"

"With farmers holding onto their heifers these days, there is a mini-shortage, and the price per pound has almost doubled. We can spare two from the herd, make some extra money to supplement the food bank with items we don't grow here."

Sweeteners and oils were the most asked-for items the food pantry didn't provide. Though not necessities, they enhanced the ability to turn the basics, such as grits or ground corn, into more palatable foods. He couldn't imagine life without the luxuries they enjoyed, including the cornbread Jacob had devoured.

"Yes, sir. They'll pull in a good chunk of change."

Taking heifers to market meant the truck and the golf cart would make the trek to the auction and market day. There'd be double loading duty, as he'd need to help Dad corral and load the heifers, as well as help Mom pack the golf cart. Not unusual, and everyone helped, but he felt out of sorts after last night. Or maybe just the thought of all three teenage girls surrounding him was too overwhelming.

"I'll get my whittling and Mr. Jenkins's beef loaded first thing after breakfast. Then I can help with the heifers."

With a nod, Dad dug into his food. Caleb followed his lead.

Come to think of it, he'd see Emma today. He'd accept her advances, even if she made them in front of Rob. No more pussyfooting around. He might just man up and ask her out on a date instead of waiting for her.

Yup, that sounded like an excellent plan. He wouldn't be alone for the rest of his life. He may not deserve some sweet young thing like Olivia, but Emma was tough enough to handle his past if he ever trusted her enough to share it. Look how that faith had worked out with Rob. His former best friend knew where all his skeletons were. But Caleb was past that. Time to move on.

«»

Mr. Boswell drove the golf cart as the ladies' protector today, so Caleb could help with the heifers and deliver the weekly payment to Mr. Jenkins. Mrs. Dunwoody remained behind, but Jacob sat in the truck's backseat with Jan, chattering about lambs.

As they pulled up to the auction barn, Jacob jumped out the moment the doors unlocked with Dad engaging the parking brake. "Come on, Jan. We've got to hurry."

Jan laughed and scrambled out behind the boy. "Hold up. I'm getting there. Remember, we've got to wait for Lizzy and Renee first. They want to search for the lamb with us."

The instant her foot hit the gravel, Jacob's hand clamped onto hers, and he was pulling her toward the animal pens. The pair could have grown up together. He was so attached to her, and vice versa. As they walked away, Caleb's heart warmed at the memory of her protecting the boy after accepting him into her life. Pretty cool to see a strong relationship that started out so rocky.

Dad stood at the back of the trailer as the heifers carried on, eager to be out of the moving vehicle. So Caleb sprinted to join him and help open the gates to the trailer and the holding pens to coordinate the transfer of the animals into the auction process.

Once they'd offloaded, they closed the gates.

Dad slapped Caleb's back. "I'm going to park the truck, and then I've got to connect with some of the other farmers before your mom arrives and needs help to set up the tables. Why don't you get the receipts handled for the heifers, then keep an eye out for the sale? Hopefully, we'll get the prices I'm looking for."

Nodding, Caleb headed for the auction arena. There weren't many animals today, and as Dad had predicted, the bulk of them were steers. A good sign. Chances were good the prices would go high on the two heifers.

Receipts in hand and Mr. Jenkins's beef in a crate, Caleb headed into the auction pit. The usual crowd was already filing in. Mr. Jenkins, sitting in the corner with a group of farmers, waved him over. "Morning, Caleb. I've got some good news for you. I found some paint for your project."

Now that was excellent news indeed. It was time to get the painting done, and he hadn't expected to have actual paint to put over the primer anytime soon. Perhaps his luck was turning around, and this was a sign of good things to come. "Enough for the entire apartment?"

"Now, hold your horses there. It's not free." Mr. Jenkins spit tobacco juice into a bottle he held in his hand. "But, yes, if we can come to a reasonable exchange rate, I've got enough for the place. What's your offer?"

Well, he'd gotten into a pickle. He'd already used all his resources to purchase the materials. *And* he'd already committed his whittling projects to replenish the food pantry. What could he offer? Best to stall for now. "I'm going to get back to you on that offer. Need to run a few numbers around in my head to know where I stand."

He watched Mr. Jenkins's face for signs his attempt at sounding like a business-minded person worked. His opponent's jaw ruminated on his tobacco wad for a few mental tics. Then he nodded. "Next week, meet me here with your best offer."

Caleb couldn't contain his grin. He had an entire week to figure out what to offer, and Dad might know how much and where to get it. Today was looking better and better.

They shook on the deal, and he handed over the crate of frozen beef and took the empty crate from the previous week's payment. Then he headed up to the top of the arena to watch the auction results for the heifers they'd brought in. If the day continued in this pattern, they'd get a tidy sum for the two breeders. Life was good.

As he settled in, the auctioneer started his spiel in the rapid-fire tempo they're known for. First up was a bull that looked long in the tooth. Most likely, the farmer needed a younger bull to take over his herd. Not the best-tasting beef, as the testosterone made the meat taste gamey. The bidding was nonexistent, with no one willing to bid the first dollar on the animal.

A flash of curls caught his attention. He forgot the auctioneer as Emma caught his eye with her blue ones. She waved at him like a beauty pageant queen acknowledging her audience. It took a while for her to saunter up to him. She rushed nowhere. A tree caught in a hurricane didn't sway as much as her slim hips did as she ascended.

Oh yeah, today was looking better by the minute.

Chapter Nineteen

Caleb slid over to make room for Emma. Was it just him, or did she smell sexy today? He foisted off his best smile. "Morning."

She ran her finger down his arm, shoulder to elbow, then sat beside him, giving her hips a few wiggles. With a wink, she said, "It's more like afternoon."

Since his grin felt like it would split his lips, he must look ridiculous, so he tried to tone it down. *Play it cool.* "I've got a question for you, a silly one."

Her eyelashes fluttered, just for a second, as she gave him her full attention. "You know what they say. There are no silly questions."

How did she do that? Just the lilt of her voice made him feel hot all over. He'd better not break out in a sweat. His hands felt clammy already. "Are you attached to anyone in particular?" Shoot. That came out sounding stupid. *Fix it.* "I mean, I'd love to ask you out on a date, but don't want to get in between you and someone you're already involved with."

Her right eyebrow rose into her descending curls. "You

wouldn't want to break up a relationship so you could be with me?"

His limbs froze into lead weights. What did that mean? Was she teasing him, or did she mean she wanted him to split the bond between her and Rob?

If she wanted him to disrupt a relationship, she mustn't be happy with it. Of course, she could just be teasing. He dug his fingernails into his palms, trying to sit still and hating this game. Why couldn't she just answer the question?

"Well, I *would* love to be with you. You're the most gorgeous woman in this place."

She dramatically flipped her hair, then stood to make a show of gazing around the arena crowd. Retaking her seat, she captured him with her eyes. "I'll be shocked if I'm not the only human female in this room." The eyebrow went up once more. "Try again."

A quick reshuffle of his thoughts, and another sentence popped out. "It's hard to tell if there are any other women in the room with you beside me. No one could compare."

That seemed to satisfy her, and she squirmed closer, placing her hand on his thigh. "Well, I can't say I haven't had plenty of offers, but so far, no guy has landed his plane in my hangar permanently."

More cryptic messages to interpret. She wouldn't make this easy, would she?

Down in the pit, they'd moved his family's heifers to the sale ring. He pointed to the auctioneer who'd begun the bidding process. "I need to listen to this one. Those are from our farm."

She turned her attention to the ring holding the animals up for bid. "I don't know much about cows, but people seem pretty interested in those two."

The bidding had started and escalated rapidly as the crowd recognized the quality animals before them. The auctioneer paused his normal banter to add some commentary. "These two beauties won't last long, gentlemen. We know the stock from this farm produces quality steers with low birth weights and rapid growth. You can't get better than this for your farm."

That intensified the bidding war, and by the time the auctioneer hollered "sold," the price was double what Dad had been hoping for. The food pantry would have plenty of cash to spend on sorghum and corn oil.

Caleb fist pumped and hissed out, "Yes!"

Emma wrapped her arm around his as he lowered it. "Well then, Mr. Moneybags, you've got some celebrating to do, don't you?"

He looked into her blue eyes and enjoyed her warm body next to his. No need to tell her the money wasn't his or that they'd earmarked it for the food pantry. Let her assume what she wanted to. Feeling like the rich guy with a beautiful blonde on his arm buoyed him. "I'll say. Shall we take a walk? Perhaps we can find a trinket to splurge on."

Her eyes lit up like it was Christmas morning. "I'd been hoping someone would shop with me today." Pushing her lips out into a pout, she continued. "I've been wanting to look at some Great Pyrenees puppies forever. And I know who has some. Come on. I'll show you."

She rose from the bench, pulling him along by the arm. He had no choice except to get up. Releasing his arm, she descended the concrete stairs, and he followed, the crate forgotten.

As they passed by, Mr. Jenkins gave him a nod and a knowing wink. Caleb stood tall, puffing out his chest and lifting his chin like he'd imagined life on campus. That's right. He had the money and the girl. Today was *his* day, and he was going to enjoy it.

They walked the length of the market, reaching the end of the tables with no sign of Emma slowing. "Where are you headed? I can't leave the market for too long. Mom will need my help back at our table."

As she flicked her hair back, she grasped his hand and intertwined her fingers with his. "We're not going that far, silly." The wink she gave him almost stopped his heart. "This guy doesn't have puppies all the time, so he doesn't rent a table spot. He couldn't afford to. His van is just a bit farther."

For sure, she'd be feeling his pulse pounding in his hand. It was pounding in his head. But maybe she'd think his sweaty palms were because of the heat, instead of this weak-willed response to her attention. He'd have followed her to the moon right now if she suggested they could walk there. Her hand felt wonderful in his.

The parking lot had few large vehicles in it since most people used golf carts. Those who had electric vehicles or could afford gasoline would act as transport services, picking up and dropping off vendors with their wares before moving to the next customer. But at the edge of the lot, he saw the van she headed for, a white van with a side door. One of those all-electric versions that started becoming popular before the variant took out the supply chain.

"There he is." She pumped Caleb's hand as they got closer. "I can't wait for you to see the puppies."

Though the van was obvious, he didn't see anyone around the vehicle, nor did he see any dogs. Would they keep the dogs inside on a hot day like today? He slowed his pace. Everyone was back at the market, taking care of business. "Are you sure? I don't see any puppies. Maybe he's walking around the market with them."

Emma tugged even harder on his hand, walking backward and pulling him along. "Come on. You'll see. They're so cute."

They reached the van and moved around to the front of it. "I still don't see anything." He froze in place. Something wasn't right. "I don't think they're here."

"On the other side," she said. "Around here."

The van's door rumbled open behind him, but before he could turn, something hard struck him. He fell to his knees, shook his head to clear it. Emma stood in front of him, smiling. Why was she smiling instead of helping? He toppled to the ground. Blackness swirled around in his head, and he was out.

«»

Caleb shook his head again, trying to get the cobwebs in his brain to clear once more. He seemed to be falling into micro-naps or something. He tried to imagine a cool breeze just beyond the door he knew had to be some place.

Though foggy, he remembered his struggle to explore his prison. Emma's participation in his capture flared fresh, and his chest constricted, further inhibiting his breathing.

Then a chain rattled. Right. Bad guys outside and coming in.

20

Chapter Twenty

With little time to prepare for his captors' arrival, he'd better play possum. Or at least, a sleeping dog. He lay down, quick and quiet. Though, as loud as the chain had been, no one could've heard him. He slowed his breathing, forcing steady inhales and exhales even though his heart was pounding in his throat. Eyes closed, he did his best to relax his face to look asleep.

A creaking completed the door opening, and then a bright light flooded his closed eyes, igniting the red behind his lids.

"Caleb," a female voice said. "Wake up. It's time for breakfast."

Emma! Now he saw red of a different variety.

Don't move. Let them think you're still knocked out.

"I guess I hit him harder than I thought." A male voice.

"I told you we should've come up with another way besides hitting him."

So, most likely, there were only two of them. Good news. Only one man and a girl. And Emma was half his weight, not a formidable enemy.

She spoke again. "You probably gave him a concussion."

The man grunted as if he were climbing up onto something. Were there no steps into the building? Caleb so badly wanted to risk a peek, but his eyes were facing the light. If he opened them, his enemies would see he was awake. He'd lose the element of surprise. Dad always said the first strike was the most important one, and shock moves had the best chance for success.

The climbing-in sounds ended.

"Give me your hand," the man said. "I'll pull you up."

"I'm good, old man."

Noises followed of something being laid down on the floor, then Emma entering the building. It didn't seem as though she struggled physically as the man had, so the guy might be out of shape. That was good too. He was probably fat and couldn't run well, so getting away from them shouldn't be too challenging if they were unarmed and if he could somehow get untied.

Oops! He was furrowing his eyebrows as he schemed. Better relax them. *Nothing to worry about here, folks. Just a knocked-out schmuck duped by a set of pretty eyes.*

Idiot.

The two advanced. It sounded as though he wasn't far from the door. Oh, what he'd give right now for a quick peek.

Relax. Slow breaths.

Someone was right beside him now. Emma's soft hand touched his forehead. At least it felt like her hand and not some callused man's hand. The hand traveled over his hairline and then to the back of his head. Searching for the place he got hit?

Don't react when she touches it.

Ouch!

"Man, you hit him good, Dave. There's a goose egg on the back of his head."

Her hand moved away from the sore spot and then down to his shoulder, then his biceps.

"His shirt is soaking wet. I told you it was too hot in here. He's probably dehydrated on top of being concussed." She stood. "Nice job, jerk."

Yes. Let them argue between themselves. *The enemy of my enemy is my friend.*

"I didn't hit him that hard. And he's only been in here for a day. A little heat won't kill a young buck. Let me see."

A wisp of air accompanied her moving away from him. Grunts and huffs followed as the out-of-shape man lowered himself to Caleb's level. Then came the stench of unbrushed teeth, along with other body odors. The man's breath was in his face, so the guy kneeled close enough for a head butt. It was tempting to try, but then what? Even Emma could control a man twice her size if he was zip-tied.

No. This wasn't the right time to strike.

The man's hand moved along his head. Not nearly as gentle as hers had been. This was going to hurt.

Oomph.

The pain brought a wave of nausea.

You will not puke. You will not puke.

"Yup. Big lump back there. Go get the flashlight out of the van. It's in the glove box. There's a first aid kit in there too. Might as well get both."

Soft steps sauntered along and then landed on leaves or other debris. Continued crunching moved away. Were they in the woods? An old hunting cabin, perhaps?

The man shuffled away and then returned.

"Well, here's food and water for you, buddy. But it doesn't look like you're going to enjoy breakfast right now."

The plop of items being dropped was right next to his head. Mmm, peanut butter and bread. Not his favorite sandwich. But beggars can't be choosers, and any food would help him regain some of the strength he'd lost in the heat. Tempted to quit the charade and "wake up" to eat, he steeled himself. He couldn't give up his advantage yet.

The crunching on leaves returned, and then something landed on the floor near the opening.

"Got the first aid kit." Something rolled toward him. "And the flashlight."

She climbed up into the building once more.

It was all he could do to lie still while the man inspected his injury.

"We just need to wash the blood out of his hair and put some of that ointment on it. Not sure how old the tube is, but that stuff doesn't expire. I don't think."

A twisting, likely of a lid coming off a bottle, crackled, and then liquid poured on the back of his head. An involuntary shiver ran down his limbs with the shock of the cool water over his overheated body.

"You awake, kid?" the man asked.

If he's asking, then he isn't sure. Keep still.

"What?" Emma asked.

"He shivered. Can you shiver if you aren't awake?"

"*Really?* Ha! Haven't you ever seen someone moving when they were dreaming?"

"Oh. Yeah."

Who were these two? Mike Myers and Dana Carvey?

"I brought more water. Just get him cleaned up, and we'll

leave the door open to keep it from getting too hot in here today. Even if he wakes up, those zip ties are tight." Emma's voice continued. "I'll check on him regularly."

He endured the pain of having the lump on his head rubbed with both the water being poured on and then the ointment being applied. The nausea nearly undid him, and the sandwich smell no longer invited him.

After they completed the ministrations, the couple moved back to the door. It sounded as if they had to hop or jump down out of the building. She seemed light on her feet while his jump sounded heavy, as if he barely made it to the ground without falling.

Then crunching footsteps moved away until they were out of hearing range.

Caleb's eyelids sprang open. It was a semitrailer. One of its two doors was wide open, and he was in the woods.

He wiggled around until he once again sat himself up and leaned against the wall of the unit. At first, the action left him dizzy with another wave of nausea. But the washing of his head wound had cooled him.

They'd left behind a sandwich and a metal bottle he hoped still had water in it. His tongue was so dry.

But if he ate the food and drank the water, he couldn't fake sleep when they returned. After a moment's hesitation, he didn't care. If he didn't eat and drink, he'd be too weak to take on his abductors when the chance came.

Besides, they'd left the door open. He was still zip-tied, but there was probably a means to get those off. There had to be plenty of sharp edges on a semitrailer. He scooted over to the bottle and grasped it with his hands. It wouldn't be easy to open it, but he brought his knees up closer to his chest, anchored the bottle between them, and used his knees to hold the bottle while he twisted the lid with his hands. Figuring out the movement with his tight bindings took a bit.

At last, the cap released. He brought the bottle's mouth to his own and gulped.

Water. *Thank you, God.*

He drank greedily, though clumsily. There must be a way to get these zip ties off. The sandwich was too tempting to ignore, so he set the water bottle down between his knees, making sure it was stable before letting go. He didn't need to lose any of it to a spill.

The sandwich was dry, the bread tasteless. Who knew what they were using for flour? Oily rough-ground peanut butter was the centerpiece of the snack. The days of creamy sweetened spreads were long gone, but the food filled his belly. For that, he was grateful.

All too soon, he'd consumed the entire meal, along with every drop the bottle contained. Part of him wished he'd saved some water for later, just in case. But his more rational brain said he needed as much as he could get to refresh both body and mind. Every calorie he had would go into escaping.

Time to check out the door. Once more, he called on his inner child and inchwormed to the opening, stopping every few seconds to listen for returning footsteps.

He reached the door and found a rough spot on the lip of the container's floor. Perfect. After positioning his body at the correct angle, he began sawing the zip ties against the sharp edge. The effort made his head pound, but it was working. Back and forth, back and forth. Sweat dripped into his eyes. He rubbed his face against his shoulder to wipe perspiration onto the shirt.

"Well, hello there."

He jumped. Emma stood, hands on hips, about five feet away, smiling as if they'd just met up at the market.

He rubbed the zip ties even more furiously in a last-ditch effort.

"Hey, Dave," she said over her shoulder, then returned her attention to him. "Caleb thinks he can escape. Perhaps you need to persuade him he's somewhat delusional."

From around the door came a heavyset man, not very tall, perhaps only slightly taller than Emma. Five foot seven, maybe. If it weren't for the bat the guy was swinging, Caleb would've kept sawing away at the zip tie binding his hands. The slits formed by Dave's eyes told him it would be dangerous to continue with the escape plan for the time being.

"I'm happy to give you a lump on the front of your head if you want a matching set." Dave's voice sounded gravelly enough to fill a rock truck to the brim. Must have been a lifetime smoker. "Keep going. I'm out of form with my swing and could use the practice."

Caleb hung his head in submission and settled his bound hands into his lap. Another chance would come. No sense in fighting a battle he couldn't win. He'd save his energy for the next round. "What do you want from me?"

"That's my guy. I knew you weren't stupid." Emma stepped closer and ran her perfect finger across his thigh. "Let's get you down out of that trailer. Then we can talk face-to-face. Dave?"

She moved out of the way so Dave could take her spot. He first inspected the zip ties, giving them a yank that bit into Caleb's already sore flesh.

The assault caused a hiss to escape Caleb's lips.

"Sit on the side of the deck, feet dangling," Dave said. "And don't be an idiot about it."

Caleb followed orders and scooted over to the end of the trailer. Perhaps Dave would be stupid enough to position himself for a kick in the teeth. A guy could hope.

Dave kept the bat cocked on his shoulder, ready to swing at a moment's notice, and he backed up just enough to be out of the range of Caleb's feet as he settled on the edge. Then he nodded to Emma. "Knife's in my back pocket. Caleb here is going to stick his feet out toward you, ever so much the gentleman, and you're going to cut the ties on his ankles so he can take a stroll with us."

She ambled up to Dave, reached into his pocket, and slid out the knife, all the while keeping her focus on Caleb.

"Best get those legs out now, son. I'd hate to be forced to break one of those kneecaps." Dave gave the bat a swing, then returned it to his shoulder to cement his point in Caleb's brain. "Slowly, you don't want to hit the lady accidentally."

She might be female, but she was no lady. Regardless, Caleb stretched his legs out, extending his toes to make the point.

When Dave nodded once more at her, Emma sauntered over, reached her hands out to keep her head out of reach, and cut the zip ties binding his feet with two swipes of the knife.

The moment his feet were free, Caleb lowered them back down and stretched his muscles by twirling his ankles. Nice to have the full range of motion back after his restricted movements.

"Put your hands out," Dave said.

Caleb did as ordered, stretching his hands as far as they would go in front of him. Like a striking cobra, Dave reached out, grabbed Caleb's hands by the tie, and yanked him off the edge of the trailer. He tumbled to the ground in a heap.

"What did you do that for?" Emma said. "He could've jumped."

When Caleb right-sided himself, Dave's sneering further snagged his fat lips.

"Best to keep him off-balance. Besides—it was fun." The bat swung close to Caleb's face as the grin became toothy with delight. "Behave, young man, or we'll have a different sort of fun, you and me."

This guy was certifiable. Caleb would need to be smart about any counteroffensives he attempted. Best to play along until he figured out his next move.

"Enough." Emma waved her soft hand toward him. "Let's take a little walk, shall we?"

She strolled off, hips wiggling with exaggerated swings. He clomped to his feet and followed, the bat swooshing through the air behind him with Dave's practice swings.

21

Chapter Twenty-One

They led Caleb to a clearing where a ragtag group eyed them. A girl a few years younger than Jan, with long greasy hair, rose from the log she sat on and moved to the circle's opposite side. She eyed them as if she expected him to attack. She'd tucked a black T-shirt into jeans that hung off her a size or two too large. A hole gaped in the collar where the seam appeared to be falling apart.

A boy about Jacob's age stood near the fire, poking it with a stick. His wild mop of hair probably hadn't touched a brush in years. The greasy mess made Caleb's head itch.

The third child was even younger, and its gender eluded him. Maybe a girl, though? A once-yellow scrunchie held her long hair as she scuttled behind the older girl.

"Have a seat." Dave pushed him down onto the log.

Emma moved between him and the wide-eyed children. "Meet the family, Caleb."

Then, as if she were a beauty pageant announcer, she introduced each, beginning with the oldest. "This is Kate." She tilted her chin toward the girl. "And Benjamin is next.

Charity"—she gestured behind her to where the youngest hid—"is the shy one."

Caleb shifted on the log, unsure of what to do. It didn't seem appropriate to put out a nice-to-meet-you vibe, so he nodded instead.

A rough jab came from behind him. Dave whispered in his ear. "The kids deserve respect. Better show it."

Caleb looked Emma in the eye. "While I enjoy meeting the neighbors, it seems odd that you'd drag me out into the woods and tie me up to meet the family."

She patted Kate's arm. "Why don't ya'll collect some more wood for the fire?" Then her curls bounced as she peered just past his shoulder. "Dave, can you go with them?"

Dave stepped around the log to stand between them. "Don't think that's a good idea."

Pulling another set of zip ties from her back pocket, she walked over, kneeled, and hog-tied Caleb once more.

She swayed side to side as she stood. "I think he'll behave for a few minutes, don't you?"

Dave grunted. "Come on, guys. The first one to find six pinecones gets to see what I brought back from the market yesterday."

"I want to stay with Emma," Charity whined.

"Me too," Benjamin chimed in.

"Unless you want to go to bed without supper tonight, you'd best be in the woods by the time I count to three." Emma didn't even look at the children, but they filed into the woods, Dave trailing.

She crossed her arms, shifted her weight to one side, and puckered her lips as though trying to decide what to say next. So he spoke first. "I guess the date's off then, huh?"

A sneer formed. "Good one, but yes, there won't be any date." She moved to the opposite side of the fire and sat on a log. "You stopped playing the game. All you had to do was bring a bit more beef over to the food pantry and let us in. No one would've been any the wiser for it, and you'd still be sitting pretty in that cushy home of yours."

That explained a lot. She was behind the blackmail all along. But why target him? "Why are you doing this? What did I ever do to you?"

"Those children, they're innocent, Caleb." Her eyes flashed. "They don't deserve what happened to them."

Huh? What did *that* mean? What could he possibly have done to these kids? He'd never even met them. "I don't understand."

"Of course, you don't." She waved a hand, her soft lips hardening. "Everyone in town thinks your family is this wonderful Christian example. You work so hard on your farm. Started up a food pantry to help the poor. Such great people."

As she spat out the last sentence out as if the words tasted poisonous, a smolder in his chest threatened to burst into flames. No one could put his family down. "So what? We work hard. My parents planned for years to be self-sufficient. Long before the variant took out the supply chains. Why should you look down on us because we're successful?"

She jumped up and paced. "Do you know whose those kids are? They're mine."

That wasn't possible. There weren't enough years between her age and even the youngest for her to be the parent. "I don't believe that for a second."

Her pacing stopped, and she spun toward him, her hair a tangle around her neck. "They're mine to raise because you killed their parents. Don't they look just like me, Caleb? You killed *my* parents."

The shock rumbled through him. How could anyone accuse him of killing these children's parents? Someone had been lying about him.

Then he relaxed. This was all a big misunderstanding. He just needed to explain she had the wrong guy. "I think you're mistaken. I've never even seen these kids, much less killed their parents. You've got me mixed up with someone else."

She grabbed a pinecone resting near the fire and threw it at his head. He ducked, and it flew past. "My father and mother were with the group that went to your farm earlier this year. They're my siblings, or they were. Now that our parents are dead, killed on your farm, I've got to be their mother and father. *Your* family tore *my* family apart. Now you're going to pay for your sins."

He froze. The marauders. Her parents had been two of the ones who'd attacked the farm. The trap his family had set had killed a handful of the gang members when they ignored the warnings to turn back. They'd blown through two signs and the first trip wire that set off a shot. Unfortunately for them, the second trap was deadly. Her parents must have been among those killed. Either that, or her father was the man who'd held Mrs. Dunwoody at gunpoint.

He'd never imagined there were children left behind. The idea made his stomach roil. They never desired that. They only wanted to be safe and left at peace on their farm. The marauders moved like locusts plaguing the area, conquering, consuming, and then spitting out the refuse of every town they went through.

It didn't appear as though the children were aware of what

their parents had been up to. Or if they knew, they didn't understand their deaths resulted from their chosen paths. But how do you explain to a child the reality of cause and effect? Of the outcomes of life choices such as their parents had made? But he should be able to explain to Emma. Surely, she could understand.

"Your parents stole and left people dead in their wake." He made eye contact, holding on and not wincing despite their raging blue fire. She was a powerful person. She had to appreciate his position. "My family did what it had to in order to survive."

"No!" Her eyes went wild as if she were coming unhinged. "The small group of adults who stayed back with us were supposed to keep our base camp safe. Once they heard how badly the fight at your farm went, they tucked tails and ran. Thankfully, Dave stayed behind to protect us. Your family has everything. My family had nothing. Now your family is going to give what they have and support these kids."

Then she calmed, her furious eyes closed, and she took in deep breaths. When she reopened them, the smile she'd beguiled him with reappeared. "And you're the key."

Now he was doubly confused. How was he a key to solving any of this mess? Then all breath rushed from his lungs. "You're going to blackmail my parents?"

His thoughts drifted to Kacie and what he'd done. Now it was going to be out there in the worst way possible. If he'd manned up and confessed, his parents could have kept it quiet. How would she tell them now? He could picture his mother sobbing into his father's chest. The idea sickened him, and his heart raced.

Her smile uncoiled as she sauntered toward him. "Not quite.

That little secret is between you, me, and the fence rail. I'm going to make it much simpler. If your parents want you back—and they seem to like you—then they'll need to pay me what I'm asking."

She moved behind him, and her hand trailed along his shoulder, then into his hair. Bending next to his ear, she whispered. "And if I return you to them—and that's a big *if*—you'll continue to pay me what I'm asking for to keep your secret quiet. Won't you?"

Gentle laughter followed.

This nightmare was worse than the ones that came in his sleep. It wouldn't end. He'd never be free, and his family was going down with him. All because of him. All his fault.

«»

Caleb woke, propped against the log he'd been sitting on earlier. Darkness loomed, and the children sat around the fire, the young boy once again poking at the flames with a long stick.

His head ached, and his parched throat begged for water. A concussion was most likely the issue since he kept drifting in and out of sleep. The weight of hopelessness settled in his chest. There had to be a way out of this—a way to protect his family.

The ties bound him in place, and Dave paced the perimeter of the camping area, going in and out of the woods. How could Caleb get free and return to his family before they paid any ransom to these thieves?

The youngest—Charity, if he recalled correctly—sat eyeing his every move. It was like being an animal in a zoo. She got off the log and walked over to Emma, who was stirring glop in a cast-iron Dutch oven dangling over the fire on a tripod.

Leaning into her older sister's ear, she whispered something, and Emma looked over at him.

"You are a sleepy one today. Lucky for you, we've got grits left over from the last food pantry run. You get to eat tonight, just because I'm a nice person."

Dave returned to the fire. "You're going to let him eat? That's not what we discussed."

The pair glared at each other. Then she stood, moving her gaze between Dave and Caleb. "Now, now. We don't want our guest to think we're heartless. Even though he should understand what it means to be hungry, we need to keep him somewhat healthy. One peanut butter sandwich a day for a strapping young lad such as him won't cut it. Will it, Caleb?"

The words made him realize he hadn't had a drink of water or a scrap of food since the first meal. His stomach, though it wasn't growling, was beyond empty. The dizzy feeling may not only be because of the blow.

Best not to agitate her. Mom always said he should be grateful for anything someone gave him. "Thank you. I would appreciate some food and water, please."

She smirked at Dave, who shook his head and remained in place. "Oh, come on, Dave. We don't want to kill the fellow. His death would ruin all our plans."

"Hmph." He picked up a canteen, brought it over to Caleb, and dropped it in the dirt in front of him.

He grabbed the canteen, unscrewed the lid with clumsy bound hands, and guzzled. The water was a balm on his burning throat.

But now, the canteen was empty, and his stomach growled. Thoughts of what was in the pot claimed his attention.

"Emma, I'm hungry." Benjamin stared at dinner. "Isn't it

done yet?"

She refocused on the boy and the pot, her smile for him a genuine greeting, such as Caleb would expect her to give someone she loved. He'd never seen such a look from her before. "Let's check it, shall we?" she said.

«»

Caleb couldn't sleep, strange as it might seem. All day, he'd struggled to stay awake, and now, he couldn't get his brain to shut off. Dave had driven a spike into the ground and tied Caleb to it tight enough to keep him from being able to move his hands much at all. It was an uncomfortable position. He could sit up as long as he was directly over the spike, or he could lie down next to it.

The others slept in bags around the fire ring. Dave lay between him and Emma and her family. Charity curled up next to Emma, and her quiet snores drifted from where she lay.

It had to be late into the evening by now, or perhaps early in the morning. It was hard to tell for sure. His head still ached, and it tempted him to indulge in sleep. But slumber would get him no closer to an escape.

A rustle sounded from behind him, deep in the woods, and drew closer. At first, he assumed it was a squirrel, but the closer it came, the larger it sounded. Probably a deer. Hopefully not a wild pig or a coyote. He craned his neck, but the bindings kept him from peering over the log.

Then came footfalls that could only be human. Was this a good sign? Someone coming to rescue him? Or a bad sign? Another one of the gang members joining Emma and Dave?

22

Chapter Twenty-Two

Deciding not to alert Dave and Emma, Caleb feigned sleep as the steps slowed. The person approaching sounded as if he or she were just on the other side of the log. Hot breath was next to Caleb's ear as someone leaned over the log. The smell of stale alcohol wafted to his nose, and it was all he could do to ignore the presence hovering above him.

A hand wrapped around his mouth to silence him, but before he could react, the invader whispered in his ear, "Don't say anything. It's me, Rob."

Caleb's eyelids shot open, and there was his best friend, standing over him. A breath of relief whooshed out of his mouth, and he closed his eyes to steady his pounding heart. When he opened them back up, Rob had stepped over the log and kneeled beside him.

Was Rob too drunk to notice the people who slept not ten feet away from them? Using his eyes, Caleb tried to direct Rob's attention to where Dave and Emma's family slept. Over and over, he looked their way and then back at his friend. But

Rob didn't seem to get the memo, no matter how Caleb tried to send it.

He let out a frustrated moan.

Rob put his finger over his own lips and whispered, "Shh."

Great. He knew enough to be quiet, but not astute enough not to sit right out in the open. Best to try a different approach.

Caleb lifted his hands the two nanometers he could and looked at them. Perhaps Rob would understand the need to release him. A questioning look came into Rob's eyes. So Caleb nodded toward his feet next, raising them for his friend to see they were bound.

Rob just looked down, as if flummoxed.

This was beyond stupid. Rob had to be toasted out of his mind. How'd he even find his way out here, anyway?

Out of nowhere, movement appeared in Caleb's peripheral vision. When he looked over, his heart practically jumped out of his chest. Emma stood over them both. "Done fooling around, Rob?"

Rob's face fell. "I was just having some fun at my old friend's expense."

Caleb's eyes flew wide open as Rob stood next to Emma. She tapped her cheek with her perfectly manicured finger, and he dutifully kissed it, then wrapped his arm around her waist.

The depth of betrayal slammed Caleb's chest. Visions from their years of friendship flashed through his brain as if he were replaying a home movie, trying to figure out where it had gone off the rails. His brain stuttered. All he could croak out was one word. "Rob?"

Emma laughed. "Pretty neat trick, huh?"

Rob's hearty laugh followed hers, which woke Dave, who joined the pair staring down at him.

"Everything okay here?"

"We're good." Emma waved him off. "Go on back to sleep."

Dave went back to his sleeping bag while Emma and Rob took seats on the log.

Caleb squirmed his way back to a sitting position, hunched over the stake where his hands remained tied.

Rob kissed Emma's cheek with no prompting this time, then chuckled at Caleb's predicament.

Emma's satisfied smirk burned like she'd driven that stake into Caleb's heart. "How did you think I knew about Kacie? Your friend here told me all about her and what you did. So, you don't even have one friend in the world who's going to back you up. How does it feel to be all alone in the world?"

There wasn't a word to describe it. He closed his eyes and let his head sink back down to the ground in utter defeat. "You win."

A foot nudged him in the ribs. "What?" Rob said. "We didn't hear you."

Not even opening his eyes, Caleb responded, "I said I give up. Why are you doing this, man? We've been friends forever. What did I ever do to you?"

The second nudge was more of a kick, but this time, his biceps were the foot's target. "What did you do? The same thing you've always done." Rob's words slurred, but anger fueled them. "Mr. Perfect, always have to show everybody else up. The girls fall at your feet, and you don't even notice. All I needed was a little help occasionally, but you didn't even have time to get me beans to plant. Did you?"

Emma took over. "Your whole family is that way, acting all godly Christian, starting a food pantry, and posturing like they care. But you're just showing off how rich you are. Now I'm going to be the rich one, and my babies are going to eat like kings while yours go hungry."

Heat powered through him, and he jerked his body into a sitting position again. "My parents worked hard on that farm for years before the variant." Somehow, he had to make them understand. His family didn't deserve to suffer for his mistakes. "Dad worked a full-time job while he built the farm. Mom did too. Jan and I worked every day after school to help make it profitable. How could we have known this was going to happen?"

"Aw. Poor little rich boy." Emma kicked dirt into his face. "I've had enough of you for one night. We've got work to do. Let's go, Rob."

As their footsteps moved away from him, Dave joined them on the clearing's far side. The children slept while the adults schemed.

After a few minutes, Dave walked back while Rob and Emma continued to talk. Dave grabbed Caleb's feet and tugged hard to ensure the zip ties were snug. He did the same with Caleb's hands, causing the plastic to dig into his wrists once more.

Emma and Rob returned to stand by Dave, the flash of her white teeth grinning at him. "We've got an errand to run now. You just stay here and behave yourself. No waking up the kiddos. No fighting. No biting. No messing up the camp."

She laughed as if she thought herself funny.

"You sure this is a good idea?" Dave tilted his head, indicating Rob. "I'm not sure he's fit for guard duty."

Her smirk spread up her cheeks. "He'll be fine. We won't be gone long."

Rob's hands crossed over his chest. "Hey, I'm not an idiot. I've got this."

When she spoke again, she kneeled before Caleb. "We're headed back to the food pantry. Only this time, your parents will let us in. That is, if they ever want to see their son again, they will. You may have been too stubborn, but I saw your mama crying when she read the note I left her."

Heat flooded his body. Mom must be scared to death right about now.

"As you should know by now, I'm a pretty good pickpocket, aren't I?" She reached over and tugged at Rob's pants pocket. "I can get a note into your clothes just as easily as I can pull something out, and you were never the wiser for it, were you?"

Well, that explained how she'd gotten the note to him. So much was becoming clear tonight. If only he'd been more astute and listened to his gut instead of his ego. Now his parents would pay the kidnappers off just to get his sorry self back home. He'd messed up royally.

She hopped to her feet and ran a hand over Rob's shoulder, then massaged his neck. "All you have to do is watch him. Don't do anything stupid while we're gone. When we get back, we'll all celebrate."

Once again, she tapped her cheek, and he kissed it. Sickening. Rob was a whipped dog she allowed out on a leash. It could have been him. It would have been him if she'd wanted it. Shame stoked the flames building in his belly.

Why hadn't he confessed everything when Mom asked? If he hadn't been so intent on keeping the secret, Emma wouldn't have had leverage against him.

His plan solidified. He wouldn't let the charade go on any longer. The moment he was back with his family, he'd spill the beans.

Knowing he needed a partner if he had any hope of escaping,

he closed his eyes. *Father, I deserve nothing from you, especially no favors. But we've had a relationship since I was little and Mom taught me to pray. If you could help me get back to my family tonight, we'd all be grateful to you. But, of course, your will be done. Amen.*

«»

Emma and Dave had been gone for a while now. Perhaps a half-hour. Caleb remained silent, hoping Rob would start a conversation from the opposite side of the fire pit. So far, Rob had said nothing, just took regular sips from a flask he'd pulled from his pants pocket.

His glare softened into a frown, and then his jaw slackened as his eyelids drooped. The alcohol must be taking effect.

Caleb needed to act now before Rob fell unconscious. He whispered so as not to wake the children. "Rob."

Rob's eyelids popped open, and he craned around as if to assure himself no one had entered the camp area unbeknownst to him.

Caleb tried again. "Rob, come over here for a minute, will you? I don't want to wake the kids up."

The befuddled look warned Rob was very close to passing out. Caleb needed to hurry.

He inched his way back into a sitting position, then tilted his head toward the log behind him. "Come on. It's not like I can do anything here, man. Just come sit with me. I need to tell you something."

On unsteady legs, Rob rose, tottered over, and plopped down on the log, just out of the range of Caleb's feet.

"I didn't tell you everything about Kacie, you know that?" Caleb said. "I only told you the parts I thought you'd want to hear. You know what I mean?"

Rob's eyes were glazing over. Even so, he mumbled, "Kacie. Poor Kacie."

Caleb needed to keep Rob awake a little longer. "Yeah, poor Kacie. Do you remember her, Rob? You kind of had a crush on her too, didn't you?"

Rob's eyes widened before the alcohol took control again, closing them. He mumbled, "Sweet, Kacie. Didn't deserve... so bad."

"Yes, I know. She didn't deserve what happened. Did she?" Time to change the subject. "Hey, you remember the game we used to play? Where we'd throw our knives and see who could land them in the bull's-eye?"

A slow smile tipped the edges of Rob's lips. "Better'n you."

Caleb plastered a smile of his own on. "That's right. You always were better than me at the game, weren't you?"

Rob slumped away from Caleb, the opposite of what he needed.

"Hey, before you fall asleep on me, let's play one round. How's that sound?"

His former friend slid off the log and onto the ground. "Sleepy."

Shoot. "Not yet, man. Don't fall asleep yet. I can see the perfect target here. See it?" Huh. No response. He tried once more. "Oh, I see how it is. You're going to let me win, aren't you? I'm going to be the one chanting 'winner, winner—chicken dinner' tonight."

"Winner-winner... me." Rob's eyes opened back up, and he sat up straighter. Then he reached into his back pocket and dug out his folding knife. "Show... you."

"Yeah, show me. See the target here, by my foot."

Caleb tapped on the ground between himself and Rob.

The drunken fool was so sauced he didn't even try to open the knife. Instead, he tossed it near Caleb's feet, where he'd been tapping, then slumped over and began snoring.

Caleb lay back down and stretched his feet out as far as he could, but his toes just missed the knife by inches. He finagled his body in every way he could think of, but fell short with each attempt.

There had to be a way to get to the knife! His wrists ached from the zip ties digging further into his flesh each time he strained to reach.

The task had him so absorbed, his heart leaped into his throat when he noticed Charity, the youngest of Emma's siblings, had wandered away from her sleeping bag and was standing beside him. After closing his eyes to get his breathing back under control, he smiled at the girl.

She smiled back.

He looked down the length of his body, toward his out-stretched toes. She walked down to his feet and picked up the target of his attention. What would she do with it? If she carried it off, he didn't know what he'd do next, so he doubled down on the smile and whispered to her, "May I have that knife, please?"

She returned the grin, walked the knife over, and handed it to him. Instead of catching it, he let it slip right through his swollen and exhausted fingers. No matter—it was within reach now.

The little girl sat down beside him as he wiggled into a seated position, picked the knife back up, and after multiple attempts, opened the blade and began sawing at the zip ties. It took a long while, but he freed his hands and his feet soon after.

Relief loosened the tightness that had cramped his every

muscle. Rob continued to snore, and Charity had fallen asleep beside him, too tired to watch any longer.

"Thank you, God. Now for step two."

Chapter Twenty-Three

Acting on the next step of his plan wouldn't be easy. As he faced the dying fire, he had to choose between staying with the children, who were without adult supervision, or heading home to assure his family he was safe.

Rob's drunken snores confirmed he was neither a threat to Caleb nor supervision for the young child who'd fallen asleep beside him. What if Charity woke back up and wandered into the woods, looking for him? He couldn't have that on his conscience.

But he could… He scooped Charity up in his arms, walked over to where Kate and Benjamin slept, and laid her beside her older sister. Then he shook Kate's shoulder with a gentle nudge. Her eyelids fluttered, then sprang open as she gaped wide-eyed at him.

"It's okay. I won't hurt you." He backed away and put his hands up, palms out, to show he was no threat. "I need you to keep an eye on your sister. Don't let her wander off."

Kate realized Charity was lying beside her and covered the younger girl with her arm, shielding her from Caleb.

Good enough. Now time to get home.

He stood and thought before heading in the direction Rob had come from. Although he didn't know his friend anymore, one thing remained certain—Rob was no woodsman. That guy could get lost in a grocery store back when the world was still normal. He couldn't even keep left and right straight in his head, much less north and south.

There had to be some sort of path or another easy way for Rob to get from his house to wherever this place was. Caleb just had to find it. As he headed away from the clearing, he prayed. "Father, me again. Thank you for helping me to get free. I need to get back to my family. I appreciate the full moon tonight. Help me find the path. Amen."

Funny how, when the chips were down, prayer seemed to come naturally. He'd need to talk to Mom about that and so much more when he was with her again.

Finding the path, a well-worn game trail sprinkled with deer droppings here and there, didn't take long. Footprints from human shoes intermingled with the tracks.

He'd probably walked five hundred yards when the trail opened to an old logging area. Here, the graveled drive the loggers created was most likely where Emma and Dave kept the van parked. Even at night, he knew where he was now. His captors hadn't moved far from where the marauders had last camped at the Boswells' home. After a few miles of hiking, he'd be home.

The question was, should he go back to his house or head to the food pantry? Emma and Dave headed to the food pantry to collect the ransom. Since they had the van, he couldn't catch up to them on foot. They were probably already on their way back now. Best to hightail it off the road into the woods.

It was a quick walk to the food pantry from his house, so he headed home first. If his parents weren't there, he'd go to the food pantry.

The ability to break into a jog freed his mind to think. Though stiff and sore from being tied up, his muscles propelled him along the edge of the woods as he watched the road for any signs of the van.

As he reached the end of the family's half-mile-long driveway, the thought of being back in the living room with his goofy sister and his parents spurred him into a full run. By the time he approached the laundry room door, he was sucking in air in huge gulps.

Home. He'd made it home safe.

Not waiting to catch his breath, he heaved open the door and charged into the house, hollering, "Mom… Dad… Jan?"

He'd not made it to the living room before Jan barreled down the stairs, screaming, "Caleb, I'm here."

They grabbed each other in an embrace that brought him to tears, crushing each other and then laughing at the joy of reunion.

Mrs. Dunwoody came rushing down next. "Caleb? Is that you?"

The moment she arrived, he pushed back away from Jan. "Where's Mom and Dad?"

Jan's eyes went wide. "They're at the food pantry. The note said they had to leave food there if we wanted to get you back alive. But they didn't go alone. The police are there too, with Mr. Tilbrook and Mr. Boswell backing them up."

"I'm going to run over. You ring the bell on the porch. Ring it for all it's worth. That way, they'll know something's up."

They both took off. Her for the front porch, and him for

the side door, heading out to the food pantry. Having had just enough of a rest to get a second wind, he broke into a half run, half jog. Soon Max and Luna found him and ran beside him, excited to be a part of the fun.

By the time he broke into the clearing of the food pantry's yard, he'd missed all the action. The van was there, Emma and Dave zip-tied and tucked into the back seat of the police officer's truck.

Max and Luna jumped and barked, huge dog grins on their faces as they ran to greet Caleb's parents as if they were shouting, "Look who we found!"

Everyone turned at the commotion. The moment his parents saw him, they ran and met him halfway. More crushing bear hugs as the three reunited. Mom was crying fresh tears over her already swollen features, and though not crying, Dad's eyes were red in the light of the police truck's headlamps.

"Thank God, we have you back." Mom pulled away and inspected his limbs for injuries. "How did you get away?"

"I'll tell you all about it later, but first, I need to tell the police about Emma's family."

"Family?" Mom's brow furrowed, and her eyes crinkled.

"Yes. First, I need a drink of water." His parched throat burned to remind him of his long trek. "Then we need to get some help to these kids."

«»

The sun was turning the skyline orange by the time Caleb, Dad, and the police officer arrived at the camp where the children hid. "It's just a bit further to the clearing," he told the officer who trailed him.

The officer put a hand on Caleb's shoulder to slow him. "Let me go ahead in case your friend is awake."

Chances were slim Rob would be awake yet, and indeed, they found him still snoring. The officer nudged Rob to see just how asleep he was, and when Rob rolled over and continued snoring, the officer moved to check on the other three occupants.

Kate awoke with the intrusion into their camp and pulled Benjamin and Charity closer to her, which woke them both. None of them said anything, but sat wide-eyed, staring.

The officer bent low in front of them, speaking in whispered tones. Though Caleb couldn't hear what the officer said, it must be comforting because soon all three siblings were smiling.

After the officer waved Caleb and his dad over, he explained. "I think you already met Caleb here, and this is his dad, Mr. Worthington. Now I trust them, and you can too. Just wait with them a minute while I talk to Rob over there. Okay?"

The kids gave no response but directed their wide eyes at Rob sleeping on the other side of the fire pit.

The officer moved over to Rob again, this time applying zip ties to his hands before rolling him over. This action brought him out of his stupor. "Hey. Stop that. Wait. Untie me." Then delayed realization hit. "No... Caleb. Tell him we're friends. I was just joking with you, man. Tell him."

"I don't even know you anymore." Caleb's chest tightened at the thought of his friend's betrayal. "You need to go dry out. Once you get that figured out, we'll talk."

The officer hoisted Rob to his feet. "Let's get you up, son. We're going to take a trip into town."

While Rob continued his protests and Caleb ignored him, Dad crouched before the siblings. "We're going to walk out to our truck. Do you need anything right now? We can come back later to get the rest of your belongings."

Charity held a dirty baby doll she hugged even closer. Kate shook her head. Benjamin grabbed the stick he'd been poking at the fire with and then kicked dirt over the smoldering ashes.

"I guess that's it then. Follow me," Caleb said.

The officer pushed Rob ahead of him, marching him back to the clearing where the police truck waited. Another officer had already taken Emma and Dave to the station.

"We'll take the kids back to our place and feed them," Dad told the officer once they reached the clearing. "They'll be safe until you determine what happens next."

«»

As they pulled up to the house in the truck, Caleb listened while Dad spoke to the three children huddled together. "We're going inside to get some breakfast while your sister talks to the police. It'll be okay. I promise."

Kate sat between Benjamin and Charity, her arms encircling them. With a nod, she grasped each by the hand and whispered to them. "It'll be fine. Let's get some breakfast while we wait for Emma."

Dad ushered them into the house, then to the kitchen where Mom and Mrs. Dunwoody talked, drinking tea. Caleb trailed.

Mrs. Dunwoody was just finishing a sentence. "…I can't believe they just left those children alone in the woods."

The moment Mom saw them, she sprang into action. "Well, hello there. Welcome. I'll bet you're hungry for breakfast." She tried to pat Benjamin on the head, but when he ducked out of reach, she continued. "Do you prefer eggs and potatoes or grits for breakfast?"

None of them responded, but Benjamin tipped his head up at Kate, eyes wide in a secret question only they knew.

"Okay then." Mom grinned. "We'll just make some of each, and you can choose whichever looks better."

She was always at her best when she was taking care of someone. It didn't take long for her to coordinate with Mrs. Dunwoody to get breakfast started and the kids' hands washed up before she shuffled them off to the dining room with Dad to entertain them.

Exhausted and filthy after living in the sweatbox for a day and then lying on the ground for a night, Caleb put his arm around his mother as he passed through the kitchen, taking a cornbread muffin from a serving plate. "Mom, I'm going to shower. But we need to talk later if you have time."

She turned from the stove and hugged him to her. "We've got a lot to discuss. And I'm hoping you'll do most of the talking."

It was time. First, a shower so he could feel somewhat human again. Then Kacie's story.

24

Chapter Twenty-Four

The shower revived Caleb, but only after he'd allowed himself to stand in the steaming heat until his skin reddened. He needed to cleanse not only his body but also his soul.

How did he even start the conversation? What words could explain the torment he'd suffered these past four years? The thought of confessing to his parents was hard. They'd never be able to see him as their innocent son again.

Dressing in his bedroom, he surveyed the items he'd collected along the way as he'd grown up. The trophy from his fifth-grade field day event, best all-around athlete. The basketball the coach had given him after he sank the winning shot in his sophomore year's regional game. The ASU pennant from the first Hornets game Dad took him to. The photo of him and Rob fishing off the River Walk in Columbus before the variant changed the world.

He knew memories collected along the way, represented by things in the physical world. Even if you took away the mementos, the reminiscences would remain. That's how life worked. Perhaps dreams and nightmares were more of the same. Lingering recollections to act as placeholders to mark time and process the memories.

A voice in his head prompted him. *It's time, Caleb.*

Time to address his guilt and acknowledge the past. Time to move on to the next stage of the grieving process.

When he arrived in the living room, Jacob and Jan had returned from their morning chores and were deep in discussions about farm life with Kate, Benjamin, and Charity.

"You've got to see the baby lambs we bought at the market," Jan was telling Kate. "Jacob and I are going to raise them, and they'll have more babies next year."

"I want to pet the lamb." Charity tugged on her older sister's grungy shirt. "Can I have one too?"

Their conversations continued as he headed to the back porch, his best thinking spot, overlooking lush pastures where cows, steers, heifers, and somewhere, Tony the bull, grazed. Caleb didn't spend nearly enough time appreciating all they had. Emma and many others like her had so much less, and forgetting that fact was too easy.

As he assumed, not long after he walked out of the house, his mother followed. She'd brought her embroidery project with her. It appeared close to completion, with most of the fabric covered in dark threads.

She sat on the bench and patted the seat beside her. Her wobbly smile didn't quite reach her eyes. He complied, and the moment he'd settled in, she spread what appeared to be a pillowcase across their laps so he could see the words she'd embroidered on it.

"I've been working on this for a while now. I've known you were struggling with something. Moms always know." She slid her arm around his and pulled him close. "This verse kept coming to me as one you needed, but I still don't know why. It's time for you to explain it to me."

She traced a finger over the words in black thread—*Therefore confess your sins to each other and pray for each other so that you may be healed. The prayer of a righteous person is powerful and effective (James 5:16).*

As he read it, a traitorous tear had the gall to escape, but he swiped at it without mercy. Head lowered and eyes focused on the words. It hurt to think, much less to speak. He was glad Mom was the one sitting with him now. Her gentle way eased his twisting gut as she placed a hand on his. What would he ever do without her in his life? Would any woman ever measure up?

She lifted her hand to his chin, then turned his head to face her, eye-to-eye. Her voice was gentle when she spoke. "Confession isn't about beating yourself up. It's about owning up to what happened, understanding your role, and then letting forgiveness take over."

He closed his eyes, desperate to keep her from seeing into his soul and uncovering the muck surrounding it. It was all he could do to choke out the words. "How can it help when I know how disappointed you'll be with me? It will hurt, and you'll suffer just like I am. That's not fair to you."

Her hand slapped his face, gentle but firm, and his eyelids popped open to see the fire in hers. "You think your family isn't already hurting with you? Wake up, Caleb. What affects you affects us all. The least you could do is tell us why we're all suffering."

An involuntary laugh exploded from deep within him. She was right, as always. How could he have been so stupid to think he was suffering in isolation? *Idiot.*

It was time to tell the story.

"You remember Kacie, don't you?"

She nodded, eyes turned up to the ceiling as if remembering. "Of course. How could I forget that sweet girl? You two were friends since kindergarten. I always thought you had a childhood crush on her. If I recall, you said you were going to marry her when you were in the first grade." They both chuckled. "It was so sad how she died."

The laughter evaporated.

"It was more than a crush, Mom. Way more."

He couldn't look at her anymore. A half-done wolf whistle howled at him from the side table along with his whittling set. Grasping the piece, he selected a detailing tool and dug into the wood that covered the animal's face.

Talking was easier when his hands had something to do.

"Go on."

"In church youth group, we were always told to wait until we were older to date one-on-one. Remember? They only encouraged group activities."

"I remember."

"We waited, Mom." The memory hurt to this day. "Until we didn't."

He paused to see if his mother would react. When her eyes narrowed in confusion, he continued.

"Do you remember the year we won homecoming right before Kacie died? It was the first time I went to the after-party? Remember, it was supposed to be at Todd's house?"

Mom put her hand on his back and rubbed slow circles. The connection warmed his skin and eased the pain. "I remember. I was so nervous that night. You stayed overnight at Rob's afterward."

He didn't dare make eye contact now, because it hurt, like a blow to his stomach to remember the lie he'd told.

"The party was at Josh McNeil's place. His parents were out of town."

Anger burned him again with the memories of the beer kegs, the bongs passed around, and what someone had slipped to Kacie. Caleb's fingers clenched on the wolf whistle, his whole body almost shaking. Kacie refused to listen to him, too influenced by the drug.

He stood and threw the wolf whistle as hard and far as he could off the back porch. It almost reached the fence to the pasture. Well, that was stupid. But releasing it—releasing the *anger*—felt good. He sat back down and picked up the pillowcase, running his finger along the words.

"I take it inappropriate things went on at the party?"

Mom was trying to get him to finish the story. This was the hard part. Time to push through it.

"Yes. They had a keg of some nasty-tasting beer, hard liquor, pot… and someone at the party had drugs. Ecstasy." He rubbed the back of his neck, avoiding eye contact. "I dodged all of it. I knew you'd be mad. Someone talked Kacie into trying the pills, though."

Then she'd been so happy, giddy beyond belief. It had almost tempted him to try it himself. She was having so much fun dancing and teasing him with her wiggling hips.

Mom brought him back to the present. "What happened?"

He sprang to his feet again and leaned over the railing. Seconds passed as he gulped in the air he needed to push the words out. His grip on the railing tightened. "She kept after me, Mom. I knew better, but I loved her. And she loved me.

She was kissing my neck. My lips. Rubbing her hands all over me." He dropped his head to his chest and barely whispered. "I gave in. We did it."

A sniffle behind him let him know Mom was in tears. He knew she would be. He'd let her down. He'd let Kacie down.

His best friend since they'd met that first day of school. She was wasted and didn't know any better. He should have been strong enough for the both of them. But he hadn't been.

Now wasn't the time to stop, though. That hadn't been the worst of it.

"Afterward, I walked her and her friend, Lisa, over to Lisa's house. They were both still pretty wasted, but we snuck them in while her parents slept. Once I knew they were safe and passed out in their beds, I left and went to Rob's house for the rest of the night."

If he could turn back the clock, he wouldn't have just tucked her into the pull-out trundle bed that night. He'd have taken her home and confessed to her parents what he'd allowed to happen. But it was too late for honesty now.

Mom cleared her throat, and when he turned to her, she patted the bench beside herself. He sat back down and scrubbed a hand over his face, but he couldn't wipe the rest away. "When we saw each other the next day, she admitted she didn't remember anything about the party. The drugs had her so wasted that the memory of her first time, *our* first time, was gone. I didn't want her to know I'd been too weak to protect her from myself. So I didn't tell her what happened."

"Oh no." Mom's comment, just above a whisper, sliced through him, and she moved her hand to her mouth as if to stop any more words from escaping.

Best to get the rest out. "It was a while later, probably a

month and a half after the party. She said she had to talk to me—needed my help."

Another tear was threatening to escape, but he fought it back. Why did he have to blubber like a baby?

Mom must've recognized how hard the story had become to share. Her hand returned to his back, soothing him. "Go on."

"I agreed to meet with her after school." His throat seemed to swell, snatching any words that threatened to come out next. Dropping his head into his hands, he sucked in a deep, steadying breath. It was so hard to finish.

Mom always stood up for him and Jan. He loved that about her. Someone was always in his corner, someone who loved him no matter what. Even when he did the wrong thing as a child, she might punish him, but she always loved him. Time to break her heart.

He shuffled his feet through the wood shavings, pushing them off the edge of the deck little by little.

"I waited for her at the football stadium after school before practice. I'd gotten dressed for practice early, so we'd have time to talk before it started. When she got there, she'd obviously been crying." He sucked in a deep breath. "She told me she'd been sick. Then she said she was pregnant and asked me if we'd done anything we shouldn't have that night at the party."

Again, the memories felt too real. It was as if he were standing in front of her again, watching the tears roll down her cheeks.

"She didn't remember, Mom. All I could think of was myself. I wasn't ready to be a father. I was going to college. I was going to play for ASU, not change diapers." His voice dropped to a whisper then, as if the air in his lungs had completely escaped and there wasn't enough left for the words. "I lied. I told her we hadn't done anything, that she must have hooked up with someone else after I'd left."

Mom sucked in a quick breath. "Oh, honey."

She stood, likely wanting to comfort him, but he held his hand up, waving her off. He needed to finish. She returned to her seat.

"I didn't help her, Mom. I should have, but I didn't. 'I have to get to practice.' I said that to her and then walked away. She was sobbing, Mom, and instead of being a man, I turned my back on her and went to practice."

He stole a glance at his mother and saw tears streaming down her face. Best to finish up and deal with her disappointment.

"The next morning, in homeroom, I learned she'd hung herself in her bedroom that night. We'd been friends since grade school. I claimed that I'd loved her and then made love with her. But when she needed me the most, I left her alone, abandoned, ashamed." He braved facing his mother, ready to accept her punishment, whatever it might be. "It's my fault she killed herself... and our baby."

His mother jumped off the bench and grabbed him in a tight hug. "You can't undo the past, Caleb. You made a mistake, but so did she. No way could you have known what she'd do."

A long while passed before he could compose himself enough to speak again. "I dream about her all the time, Mom. It's like she's haunting me, reminding me of what I did wrong."

"I knew her death affected you." She spoke into his ear in a hoarse whisper. "But I didn't realize how much. We should've taken you to a grief counselor. I'm so sorry I didn't realize."

Wasn't that just like his mom? He admitted to having sex at a party with a girl who wasn't in her right mind, and Mom wanted to comfort him instead of reading him the riot act.

"I talked a lot about it to Rob. He was the only one who knew what I'd done. That was the one weapon he had against me, and so it was a great tool for him to share with Emma."

Mom backed away from him, a confusing fury in her eyes. "You listen to me, young man." She waved a finger in his face. "Failures are not weapons we use against people. Grace is the only weapon Christians should be using. And that weapon is one *for* people, not against them."

Grace. How could she be talking about forgiveness at a time like this? "Mom, I don't deserve grace. I abandoned Kacie when she needed me the most. No one could have failed her any more than I did."

"Don't you get it, son? None of us *deserves* grace. That's the point." She placed her hand on his arm. "What happened to Kacie is terrible. Maybe you could've helped her if you'd fessed up that night, and maybe not. You've learned from your mistake, haven't you? Would you do things differently today if you knew then what you know now?"

"Yes, ma'am. I certainly would." He closed his eyes again. "I wish I could do it all over again." He'd wished he could take back his response as soon as the shock of her pregnancy wore off. He was going to tell her everything when he saw her at the school the next day. But she'd never come in. He'd never seen her again.

Mom placed her palm on his face, getting him to open his eyes and see her once more. "All we can ask of ourselves—and others—is to learn from our mistakes. That's the gift grace allows us to have. Accept that gift. Accept forgiveness for yourself and let Kacie rest in peace."

It sounded too easy to let himself off the hook. He still felt the loss of her in his life. Mom was right, though. He needed to accept the consequences of his mistakes and say goodbye to Kacie.

"Yes, ma'am."

25

Chapter Twenty-Five

Exhaustion pulled Caleb under as soon as his head hit the pillow.

He walked around the football stadium, looking for Kacie. He'd agreed to meet her before practice started, but she hadn't shown up yet. Where was she? He'd be late for practice if he didn't head back to the field soon.

As he rounded the stadium seats, he saw her coming through the entrance gate. He couldn't see her face from this angle, but he could see her shoulders shaking. Was she crying?

He jogged up behind her and touched her shoulder to get her attention. She turned, surprised by his touch. Tears streamed down her face, but they were tears of laughter. That realization started him laughing as well. Funny how one person laughing can be contagious, even when you don't know what's causing it. He had to find out.

"What's so stinkin' funny?"

She struggled to gain her composure, then squeaked out, "They asked if I wanted to try out for cheerleaders this fall."

A fresh fit of giggles took over, and her poise crumbled once more.

Knowing why she was laughing so heartily, he couldn't help but join her. He'd always thought she was the most beautiful girl in the world, but their personal joke revolved around her inability to walk a straight line down the school hallways without tripping on the seams of the floor tiles. A natural-born klutz, but still his best friend since kindergarten.

As she laughed, her sandy blond hair rippled with waves flowing down her back, and her hazel eyes glowed. Those eyes were his favorite part of her. They changed colors with her various moods or clothing choices. Today, flecks of green flared in them. Gorgeous.

He needed to get back to practice soon.

"So, what did you need?"

She stifled her giggles once more and placed her hand on his. "I just wanted to say you're still my best friend. You know that?"

He couldn't suppress his smile.

"Always."

«»

The sun streaming through his window woke him. It was the first time since she'd died that he'd dreamed of her, and it wasn't a nightmare. The smile from the vision still rested on his face, and it felt right.

Jacob and Benjamin, carrying on downstairs, yelled rambunctious whoops. They must be pretending to be pirates again because an "argh" drifted up from one of them and an "aye, me matey" from the other.

After dressing, Caleb shuffled downstairs and found Charity sitting on a chair at the kitchen island. She was helping to stir the cornbread batter, or so it seemed. Mrs. Dunwoody did most of the work and steadied the large bowl to keep the young girl from dumping the batch on the counter.

Jan, Kate, Lizzy, and Renee huddled around the dining room table. With the high-pitched voices sounding like "girl talk," he did his best to avoid the room. His eye caught Renee's as she gave him a tentative smile. He returned it.

He moved to the back porch to drink in the new day and found his father already out there, leaning against the rail, watching the cows forage in the field. "Morning."

Dad waved a hand toward the pastures. "And a good morning to you as well. Ready to help with fences today? Or were you going to work in the apartment?"

Joining Dad at the rail, Caleb looked out at two calves pushing head-to-head, practicing their dominance skills. The pair took off running and jumping, enjoying their playtime. His chest warmed.

"I thought I'd work inside. I'm getting close to completion."

Dad clapped him on the back. "Would you like some help?"

He'd already told his father about Kacie, but he still needed "guy time." Finishing the additional living space would be the perfect project to work on together.

"I'd love that. It'll give us some time to talk. Before I start, though, I need to use the golf cart to run an errand."

Dad's eyebrow quirked up. "And what would that be?"

A knot in the pit of his stomach twisted at the thought of what he needed to do. "I need to go see Rob. He's been my best friend for as long as I can remember. We need to talk."

"Fortunately for you, it won't be a long drive."

The confusion he felt must have been obvious, because Dad laughed. "Jan's favorite policeman, Officer Bradley, stopped by earlier."

Caleb had to smile. Officer Bradley offended his sister, treating her like a "little lady" when they'd last needed to call the police. "Did Jan get to talk to him?"

Dad's grin widened. "Not this time, thankfully."

"Did he say anything about Rob?"

"He's already out. Emma confessed to being the ringleader of the blackmail plan and said Rob was a drunken fool who played into her hands." He ran his hands through his hair. "The police don't have enough room for people like him in jail. His parents have committed to finding someone who knows how to wean him off the booze."

"What about Dave?"

"He's a different story. Said he'd overseen keeping the kids safe when the marauders were on the prowl. As an adult, he should have kept Emma from crossing the line. Instead, he egged her on. Plus, they've connected him to other crimes he took part in with the marauders. He'll be in jail as long as they can keep the place open."

He had to hope the prison could hold offenders like Dave until society right-sided itself.

A thud from inside the house caught their attention. Jacob's voice filtered out. "Let's go see the chickens. Did you know they lay eggs every single day?"

The boy's enthusiasm brought a smile to his face. He turned his attention back to his father. "What about Emma's family?"

Dad shrugged. "Officer Bradley said they still don't have children's services running in this area. So, the kids will stay with us for a while since Emma has no other family to send them to."

Caleb's shoulder slumped at the thought of the children without parents—and now without their sister as well. "How long does he think Emma will be in jail?"

"It's hard to tell. She's confessed and seems to regret what she's done. And they don't have facilities available to hold criminals. She asked the officer if we'd care for the kids. Apparently, she trusts us enough to make sure they're fed, clothed, and protected. Strange but true."

In a weird, twisted sort of way, that almost made sense.

«»

As he pulled up to Rob's house, Caleb could hear shouting from inside.

He recognized Mr. Jackson's voice. "Why can't you act like an adult?"

Expletives flew from Rob's mouth. Talk like that would have resulted in a bar of soap firmly lodged in his mouth if it had been Caleb talking to his own mother.

It would have been nice to have been able to bring the truck. The noise of the mufflers would have alerted their neighbors to his arrival. Now he sat in the cart, wondering if he should knock at the door or return home and wait for a better day.

"No rest for the wicked," he mumbled to himself. "Better to get this over with."

The short walk from the cart to the door felt as if he were heading toward a boxing ring for the fight of his life. How had things gotten so mixed up between him and his best friend?

The moment he knocked on the door, the shouting ceased, and quiet settled over the home. It felt like he could have counted to one hundred multiple times waiting for a response from the home's occupants.

Maybe he shouldn't have come. Sometimes it's better to leave sleeping dogs lie.

The moment he'd turned to head back to the vehicle, he

heard the doorknob turn, and the door opened.

"Caleb," Olivia said as she stepped outside and closed the door behind her. "We weren't expecting you. It's not a great time for a visit right now."

"Yeah, I heard." He rubbed the back of his neck, searching for words as he walked up to her. "Look, I know he's probably a hot mess today, but I need to see him."

Behind Olivia, Caleb saw movement in the door's side window. Was it Rob? His parents?

He blew out a breath in frustration. "I'm not leaving until I speak to him."

With a quick look back at the house, she faced him once more. "I'll see if he'll talk."

She went back inside, closing the door behind her.

So, there wouldn't be an open invitation. He could understand that. But he wouldn't leave without saying his peace. He'd spent way too many hours of his life being a part of the Jackson family, and Rob being a part of the Worthington family, for the relationship to end without a fight.

And he was itching for a clash at this point. Perhaps that's what they needed. A good old-fashioned fistfight to get it all out. It had solved the problem of who got to sit beside Kacie on the bus when they were in kindergarten. It could bring this to a resolution too.

The next round of swearwords told him Rob knew he was there. Rob's voice escalated with each sentence. "Just who does he think he is? I don't report to him."

That did it. He'd had enough. The time for a courteous invitation into his best friend's house had ended.

A fire lit in his belly as he stormed up to the door, twisted the knob, and thrust himself inside as it swung open.

He knew this house like the back of his hand and from the sound of Rob's voice, knew he'd find him in the game room. Their old hangout.

Mrs. Jackson was in the living room, tears in her eyes, wringing her hands. Olivia's shocked eyes followed Caleb as he strode down the hallway to confront his friend.

When he walked into the game room, Mr. Jackson stood facing the door, glaring at Rob, who sat on top of the air hockey table. The man's face had aged ten years since the pig roast. Shocked eyes looked back at Caleb when they first connected, but soon mellowed with realization.

With a nod, Mr. Jackson walked towards the door, but stopped once he was beside Caleb. "I'm sorry, son. I didn't know."

"It's not your fault, sir."

A single glance at the older man told Caleb everything he needed to know. The anger had dissolved into sorrow as Mr. Jackson's eyes filled with tears.

As Caleb watched, the man's shoulders sagged, and he walked out of the room, somehow smaller than he'd been moments ago.

Rob still faced away from Caleb, but there was no way his friend didn't realize he was standing in the room. If Rob wanted to play these games, he was more than happy to engage today. He'd like nothing better than to get this party started.

Caleb marched over to the game table and shoved Rob hard, knocking him off the table. "What gives? Since when do you curse at your mama?"

Obviously inebriated, Rob couldn't catch himself and sprawled onto the floor. He scrambled back up, unsteady, but with a fire in his eyes as he faced Caleb. "Who invited you in? I'd have thought you'd be too busy working on that fancy apartment of yours to come slumming it over here."

What an idiot. He planted his feet and pulled himself up to his full height. Then he slowly raised his fists up in front of his face, ready to spare. "So, you want to compete, huh? Why bring our families into it? Be a man. Face me head-on, ya wuss."

An animal growl came from Rob's throat, and he charged at Caleb.

All he had to do was step aside and pivot and the drunken teen passed right by and fell to the floor once more.

Rob bellowed. It was as if every frustration since the world collapsed was being released in one howl. He charged once again. "Argh!"

With a simple pivot and a shove at the passing body, Caleb easily forced Rob to the floor once more. There was no competition. He couldn't fight with a drunk.

He stared at this friend, who panted from the floor in front of him. All the fight drained out of Caleb and the knot of despair was back in his belly. "Why? We were best friends. I'd have done anything to help you and your family. You know that."

Rob didn't even make eye contact. He curled up in a ball and muttered. "I hate you."

So that was it. The alcohol ruled, and friendship was out the window. "You need to dry out, my friend. Whenever you decide you're ready to do that, I'll be there for you." He turned and headed towards the door. "Until then, you are no longer welcome on our farm."

As he moved back to the front of the house, he saw Mr. and Mrs. Jackson sitting in the kitchen, and Olivia stood at the sink rinsing dishes. They all turned to him as he entered. The looks of despair in their collective stares were more than he could bear.

Tears welled in his eyes as he walked over to his best friend's parents and hugged each one. "I'm sorry. I wish there was something I could do."

Mr. Jackson stood with Caleb's hug and returned the embrace with a crushing enthusiasm. "Don't you worry about us. We'll get this sorted out. And when we do, you'll be the first to know."

It felt as if he were abandoning them as he walked out the door with a last nod of acknowledgment to Olivia. The door's click as he pulled it shut felt like he was closing them all into a prison cell. A jail of Rob's making that they'd all have to endure.

26

Chapter Twenty-Six

Caleb almost tripped over Charity when he walked back into the house. She sat just steps away from the door, playing with one of Jan's old dolls. They must have pulled a box of her old toys out of the attic.

He knelt to her eye level. "What've you got there?"

The look of glee in her sweet eyes warmed him inside. "Jan said this was her best doll ever. But she said I could keep her forever, as long as I take good care of her."

He ruffled her soft hair. "That's fantastic, sweetie. Where are all the other kids?"

The tiny shrug was the only response he got as she turned her attention back to the toy. She sang as she rocked her pretend baby. "Sweet little baby… you're my sweet baby… I'll take care of you all day long…"

The tune reminded him of how innocent she'd been when she helped him to escape. He hefted her up into his arms. "Come on, let's go find Mom."

Together they wandered into the kitchen where Jacob and Benjamin sat on stools at the island, helping Mrs. Dunwoody shell peas for supper. At least she was shelling peas. They seemed to eat more than they put into the bowl she was using.

He sat the small girl down on a third stool. "I've got another helper for you, Mrs. Dunwoody. I'm sure Charity would like to feed her baby some of those peas the boys are eating."

Mrs. Dunwoody smiled as she pushed a small pile of pea pods in front of the little girl. "We've got plenty to go around."

Mom's voice was coming from the dining room and Caleb headed there next.

"It'll be tight, but we'll make it," Mom said as she held Dad's hand across the table. "Sleeping bags will do until we can figure out beds."

Their attention turned to him as he stepped into the room. He shoved his hands into his jeans. "I'm back. Ready to get started on the apartment again?"

Mom's eyes crinkled with worry. He wondered if it was over Rob's complicity in the scheme to blackmail the family, or if it was more about the additional mouths they needed to feed. She patted her husband on the hand as she rose. "Well, I need to help with supper anyway. We'll finish the conversation later. I'll leave you two gentlemen to your work."

A frown marred his father's face as he got up and turned to Caleb. "Everything go alright?"

He shrugged. "Rob was drunk—again. Or maybe, as usual. But I said my peace."

"Sometimes a man's just got to get that out. Let's get to work."

They went up the stairs and passed by Jan's room. Lively chatter from the gaggle of girls on the bed emanated from the room. Kate, Jan, Lizzy, and Renee all sat on the full-size bedspread and didn't even notice when the men passed by the room.

They crowded the house with more people than it had been designed to hold. The game room was now a bedroom for Mrs. Dunwoody, Jacob, and Benjamin. Jan shared her room with Kate and Charity.

His parents hadn't built a home for a growing family. They'd built it assuming their children would head off to college in a few years and they'd need less room, not more.

The dumbwaiter moved them up into the attic space that looked more like an actual apartment every time he stepped into it.

The painting was all that really needed to be done and then it would be ready for them to move furniture into. Dad had negotiated for a used couch, a small table set, and even a microwave. It was a tiny dorm version of the appliance, but since they were running off solar most of the time, the low wattage would be a better fit for the space.

He stirred the paint in the can, prepping it for the walls. Dad started on the opposite side of the space and was already applying strokes of white to the floorboards.

Caleb let out a heavy breath. He couldn't hold back the thought that had been eating at him. "Dad, I'd like Mrs. Dunwoody to have the apartment when it's done."

Dad's eyes went wide. "Why? You've put so much into it. I thought you wanted your own place."

"Don't get me wrong, I *do* want that. But with three more people in the house, how can I justify taking up so much space? If Mrs. Dunwoody and Jacob move up there, Benjamin will go with them. That'd leave the third bedroom on the second floor free for Kate and Charity."

He looked his father in the eye, the smile there confirm he

was doing the right thing. "I can handle being in my old room a while longer. It's not like I'm getting married tomorrow or anything."

The clap of his father's hand against his back rang like the proverbial music to his ears. "I'm proud of you, son. Never forget that."

"I won't, Dad. I promise."

The End

Take a sneak peek at the next installment!
Collapse: The Death of Independence

Collapse Series Book 3: Independence
~ Chapter 1

"No, Dad. Don't leave. We can find another way." At just seventeen years of age, Olivia Jackson faced a world falling apart — again. How much sorrow was one person expected to shoulder? Wasn't it enough that she lost her mother?

Her father's expressionless face hurt her more than if he'd shown some anger. "There's no other way. I'm sorry. I can't add another mouth to feed to my brother's home."

Uncle Kevin and Aunt Amanda stood behind Olivia, facing her retreating father.

Uncle Kevin reiterated the same offer he'd made dozens of times in the last twenty-four hours. "Tom, you don't need to do this. We'll make it work."

Aunt Amanda rubbed Olivia's shoulders from behind. "Come on, Tom. Your brother's right. There's no need to split your family apart."

Dad whirled back to them, his eyes blazing. The hands he'd been wringing now jammed in his pockets, his resolve hardening. "Once I find work, I'll come back and get you. I won't have my baby sleeping on the streets. It's not safe."

"Take Olivia inside, Amanda." Uncle Kevin waved toward the door. "My brother and I need to talk."

"No!" Olivia couldn't let her father out of her sight. "I need to stay with Dad."

Her uncle's glare revealed his anger. "Amanda. Now."

Aunt Amanda pulled at Olivia's arm, steering her away.

Olivia shouted over her shoulder as she allowed herself to be drawn back toward the house. "Promise me you won't leave without saying goodbye!"

No response came from her father, and she dissolved into sobs. Aunt Amanda folded Olivia into her arms as they trudged away.

«»

It was dark outside when Olivia woke, lying atop the bedspread. Dried tears glued her eyelids shut, and a heaviness pressed her into the bed.

Though no one had told her as much, she knew her father was gone. Aunt Amanda stopped by the room multiple times, offering water, soup, a hug, anything to help ease the pain and loneliness. But the lump that settled in Olivia's chest threatened to heave up anything left in her stomach from breakfast.

When she rolled to her side, the soggy pillowcase cooled her cheek.

Now what? Not only was her mother gone, but her father as well. Abandoned. Stranded with an extended family she barely knew.

Uncle Kevin brought his family to Columbus last year, and they stayed with Olivia and her father for a few short months, trying to find work. Dad thought he could get Uncle Kevin a job at the factory. Instead, Dad lost *his* position.

They didn't stay long after that. Dad's drinking drove them away.

She got out of bed and wandered down the hallway to the

bathroom. There was no electricity tonight. Power was never a guarantee these days. Tonight, a full moon shone through the bathroom window. With the door open, it lit the hallway enough to keep her from stubbing her toes.

After using the toilet, she rinsed her hands under the faucet. There wasn't any soap. She hadn't seen soap regularly since her father lost his job, and it had been sparse before that.

Funny how she used to take minor items like hygiene for granted. Mom had been so picky about her laundry detergent. She had to have a particular scent and would stop at two or three stores if they were out of what she liked.

That was *before.* Before the variant. Before it all fell apart. Before Mom died.

Olivia dried her hands on a rough towel, inhaling a scent she wasn't expecting—vinegar. Interesting. People made do with what they had, but she'd never heard of washing laundry with vinegar. Couldn't be worse than nothing at all, though, right?

She gazed into the mirror. Though her long brunette hair looked black in the dark, her swollen eyes provided a dead giveaway to a long night of tears.

As she padded back up the hallway, she passed by her cousin's room. Mumbling came from inside as if Rob were having nightmares. They all had their demons now. *She* certainly did.

Back in her room, she slipped under the covers. The night had turned chilly, so she pulled up an extra blanket from the bottom of the bed. Even with no heat in the house, it only got cool late into the evening and early the next day. Of course, there was no air conditioning either, and the Georgia heat was harder to hide from than the cold.

Snuggling under the covers, she let her mind drift. Was there a chance she could fall asleep again? Perhaps staying awake was better anyway. She didn't want to wake up to life without her father.

Dad wouldn't be back. She didn't know how she knew, but her brain resolved it. She should be grateful he'd stopped drinking long enough to bring her to Shiloh. He'd only remain sober if he ran out of alcohol. But somehow, even when he couldn't earn a dime for a meal, he always found a way to get a drink.

If only he'd put as much time and attention into finding work. She might still have a family.

Enough!

Tomorrow, she had to face her new life. She had to make it without him now or find someone else to take care of her. Maybe Aunt Amanda and Uncle Kevin meant what they said. Perhaps they would be her caregivers.

She drifted off to sleep with the crickets chirping outside her window and her cousin mumbling nightmares in the room next door.

«»

Three months later…

"Olivia, can you please come help me?" Aunt Amanda hollered from outside the open bedroom window. "I've got the net all tangled up and can't get this bird free."

Still dressing for the day, Olivia looked out the screen and groaned. What a tangled mess her aunt had gotten into!

"I'll be right there."

She picked up her jacket and slid her arms into it. A little nippy this morning, today promised some relief from the previous day's heat. Fall eased out the oppressive summer temps but brought worries of how they would survive after the growing season.

As she opened her bedroom door, her uncle's voice emanated from the kitchen. From the low tones, he must want the conversation to remain private, so he was discussing her cousin or lecturing Rob in person.

Either way, she'd rather avoid the discussion. She quickened her pace toward the front door.

Her stomach growled. Their hard work in the garden produced limited success. Before they'd found a barrier, the deer ate every bean they planted. The second planting produced only anemically. Nothing like the Worthingtons' garden next door.

As Olivia rounded the side of the house, Aunt Amanda's brow furrowed, and her lips pressed tight. "I don't know how I got this so tangled up. I think the bird is in worse shape than when I started."

The six-foot-tall net fence kept deer out. The barrier ran around the perimeter of their plot, tacked up to poles on the four corners. A dove flapped its wings, tangled in the material.

Olivia hustled over. "I guess adding the top section to keep birds out worked. Maybe a little too well."

The fowl's frantic movements stopped as her aunt grasped it and folded its wings by its sides. A trickle of blood emanated from the tousled feathers, and Olivia cringed. She hated to see any animal suffering. Even if it was stealing their food. Sections of mesh crisscrossed its body in a hopeless tangle. "Should I get a knife or some scissors? I'm not sure how else to get it out."

Her aunt shook her head. "We can't waste the material. It took us months to find this, and who knows if we'd find a replacement if we hack it up." A long sigh escaped her lips.

"We may not save the bird. That's what it gets for trying to steal our sunflowers."

Like the trapped bird, Olivia's heart fluttered in her chest. Letting the bird die was more than she could bear. "Let me try."

Her thin fingers lifted the bird's wing, causing more flutters and cheeps. The mesh cut deep into its joint, and its feathers pulled in awkward directions.

"Come on, little one. We're trying to save you, but you need to help yourself and stay calm," Aunt Amanda cooed.

Once more, Olivia touched the tiny body and worked one square of the net off the wing, then smoothed the feathers into place. "One down. Quite a few to go."

With a sigh, her aunt nodded for her to continue.

Little by little and section by section, they spent the next half hour freeing the bird. By the time they removed the net from its feet, all three shook from strained muscles.

"Moment of truth." Aunt Amanda lowered the dove to the ground. "Let's see if you can still fly."

They released it, and the bird flew a few feet, then dropped back to the grass.

Olivia walked toward it, but before she could get within arm's reach, it flew up again and landed in a nearby oak tree. "Good enough. At least in a tree, it won't be lunch. If it's lucky, it'll get over the shock and find its way home."

Planting her hands on her hips, she faced the net. Perhaps they could salvage it. The bird's gyrations and their efforts to free it had broken some strands.

From the house, her uncle shouted, "If you live under this roof, you'll do what I say! Otherwise, you can get out."

Aunt Amanda winced and brushed her grimy hands on her

jeans. "I'd better go see if I can help."

"I'll stay here and work on this." Olivia knew better than to go inside now. "It'll take most of the morning to figure this tangle out. Good thing I like puzzles."

She smiled at her aunt to ease her burdens and received a weak grin in return. In this house, joy was scarce as food, and laughter as nonexistent as soap.

After Aunt Amanda returned to the house, a calm came over the building. At least Olivia couldn't hear anything from outside. Quiet was the most she could ask for.

Rob was a hot mess. He was lucky the prisons barely functioned these days and could only hold the most hardened criminals. Many states reinstated the death penalty for heinous crimes to keep the worst off the streets.

Her cousin wasn't dangerous. Just an alcoholic.

While Rob's recent history with a deceptive criminal added to his problems, her father was likely to blame for Rob's alcohol addiction. She wished they'd never gotten together.

Her fingers continued to unravel the knots. A rumble in her gut reminded her she'd not eaten yet. If Rob would stop drinking, perhaps the family could focus on their food situation.

Aunt Amanda didn't want to push him to go cold turkey. A local doctor advised them a sudden stop could kill him. The physician had connections to an Atlanta specialist with access to the medications to wean Rob off alcohol. But they had to wait for the drugs to arrive via courier, and that didn't happen often these days.

She arched her back and tried to stretch out the spasms in her hands. There was so much to miss from her old life. How had she not appreciated the conveniences of the daily mail,

Amazon two-day shipping, and even pizza delivery?

But more than anything, she missed her parents.

Labor Day had to be coming up soon, but there wouldn't be any picnic.

Halloween would be next, and if her mom was still alive, they'd be planning some silly costumes.

When Thanksgiving came, Mom cooked the best turkey dinner. Closing her eyes, Olivia could almost smell the savory gravy simmering on the stove, the spicy apple pie baking in the oven, and the dressing crisping to accompany the main course.

All gone.

Now she lived with a family she struggled to understand and endured their daily battle. Rob wasn't the only one who dealt with his drinking. The whole family lived it.

That struggle was on top of the need to work for every morsel of food they put on the table.

The net slowly became untangled under her fingertips. Unloop here and uncross there, stretch it out and reattach to the poles. A snail's pace, but she had nothing else to do, much less anyone to talk to. Because of her petite five-foot frame, she needed a cinder block to reach the tops of the poles, but she'd learned to be resourceful in the years since the supply chain collapsed.

When a day started like today, no one would pay attention to her. Rob's problem would absorb her aunt and uncle until he fell into bed that evening. That was a given.

If only she could visit her former friend, Jan, on their farm up the road. In the month since Rob admitted to helping blackmail Jan's brother, none of them had gone to the Worthington ranch. Though Jan's brother forbade Rob access to the farm, the other family would never forbid her contact. But embarrassment kept them apart.

How do you tell someone you're sorry your cousin extorted them to get what they had?

She missed Jan. She missed the farm. She missed Caleb. And her body missed the food they used to enjoy when they ate their communal meals.

Now she'd spend her day untangling this net to protect a sad excuse for a garden. Though Jan and her family had been teaching her how to grow food, she had so much more to learn. The jaundiced-looking produce proved it.

Why couldn't they all reconcile?

Her stomach rumbled.

A tear slipped down her cheek, and she swiped it away. How could Rob ruin everything? How could she fix it? And how long could she live like this?

She tightened her fists. Her ragged nails cut into her palms as her breathing quickened. She couldn't bring her dad back. But, surely, she could find her way in life again. Find someone to care about her and take care of her. Find a place she belonged without the pall this family cast over her.

The End

Dear reader, thank you so much for sharing Caleb's journey with me! If you enjoyed reading *Collapse: The Death of Honor*, I would gratefully appreciate you leaving a review on Amazon, Goodreads, or other sites to help others discover my books. Those minutes of your time make a tremendous difference to writers like me, not only in helping others find our books but also in encouraging us to keep up the effort of writing.

And with that thought, I hope you will enjoy Olivia's story, the next story in this series, *Collapse: The Death of Independence*, and I'd love to have you join my posse of friends. So please sign up for my newsletter at www.AngelaDShelton.com and receive a **free** gift when you sign up, or connect with me on Facebook, Instagram, Medium, and Pinterest.

See you next time! Angela